W9-CZX-492

Immigration

Other Books in the Social Issues Firsthand series:

SOCIAL ISSUES
FIRSTHAND

Immigration

Karen Miller, Book Editor

GREENHAVEN PRESS

An imprint of Thomson Gale, a part of The Thomson Corporation

THOMSON

GALE

Detroit • New York • San Francisco • New Haven, Conn. • Waterville, Maine • London

Christine Nasso, *Publisher*
Elizabeth Des Chenes, *Managing Editor*

LIBRARY OF CONGRESS CATALOGING-IN-PUBLICATION DATA

Immigration / Karen Miller, book editor.
   p. cm. -- (Social issues firsthand)
  Includes bibliographical references and index.
  ISBN-13: 978-0-7377-2893-4 (alk. paper)
  ISBN-10: 0-7377-2893-0 (alk. paper)
  1. United States--Emigration and immigration--Case studies--Juvenile literature.
  2. Refugees--United States--Case studies--Juvenile literature. I. Miller, Karen, 1973–
  JV6601.I66 2007
  304.8'73--dc22

                          2006028630

Contents

Chapter 1: Finding a Place in a New Land

Chapter 2: Adapting to the American Way of Life

Chapter 4: America's Benefits

Foreword

Social issues are often viewed in abstract terms. Pressing challenges such as poverty, homelessness, and addiction are viewed as problems to be defined and solved. Politicians, social scientists, and other experts engage in debates about the extent of the problems, their causes, and how best to remedy them. Often overlooked in these discussions is the human dimension of the issue. Behind every policy debate over poverty, homelessness, and substance abuse, for example, are real people struggling to make ends meet, to survive life on the streets, and to overcome addiction to drugs and alcohol. Their stories are ubiquitous and compelling. They are the stories of everyday people—perhaps your own family members or friends—and yet they rarely influence the debates taking place in state capitols, the national Congress, or the courts.

The disparity between the public debate and private experience of social issues is well illustrated by looking at the topic of poverty. Each year the U.S. Census Bureau establishes a poverty threshold. A household with an income below the threshold is defined as poor, while a household with an income above the threshold is considered able to live on a basic subsistence level. For example, in 2003 a family of two was considered poor if its income was less than $12,015; a family of four was defined as poor if its income was less than $18,810. Based on this system, the bureau estimates that 35.9 million Americans (12.5 percent of the population) lived below the poverty line in 2003, including 12.9 million children below the age of eighteen.

Commentators disagree about what these statistics mean. Social activists insist that the huge number of officially poor Americans translates into human suffering. Even many families that have incomes above the threshold, they maintain, are likely to be struggling to get by. Other commentators insist that the statistics exaggerate the problem of poverty in the United States. Compared to people in developing countries, they point out, most so-called poor families have a high quality of life. As stated by journalist Fidelis Iyebote, "Cars are owned by 70 percent of 'poor' households. . . . Color televisions belong to 97 percent of the 'poor' [and] videocassette recorders belong to nearly 75 percent. . . . Sixty-four percent have microwave ovens, half own a stereo system, and over a quarter possess an automatic dishwasher."

However, this debate over the poverty threshold and what it means is likely irrelevant to a person living in poverty. Simply put, poor people do not need the government to tell them whether they are poor. They can see it in the stack of bills they cannot pay. They are aware of it when they are forced to choose between paying rent or buying food for their children. They become painfully conscious of it when they lose their homes and are forced to live in their cars or on the streets. Indeed, the written stories of poor people define the meaning of poverty more vividly than a government bureaucracy could ever hope to. Narratives composed by the poor describe losing jobs due to injury or mental illness, depict horrific tales of childhood abuse and spousal violence, recount the loss of friends and family members. They evoke the slipping away of social supports and government assistance, the descent into substance abuse and addiction, the harsh realities of life on the streets. These are the perspectives on poverty that are too often omitted from discussions over the extent of the problem and how to solve it.

Greenhaven Press's Social Issues Firsthand series provides a forum for the often-overlooked human perspectives on society's most divisive topics of debate. Each volume focuses on one social issue and presents a collection of ten to sixteen narratives by those who have had personal involvement with the topic. Extra care has been taken to include a diverse range of perspectives. For example, in the volume on adoption, readers will find the stories of birth parents who have made an adoption plan, adoptive parents, and adoptees themselves. After exposure to these varied points of view, the reader will have a clearer understanding that adoption is an intense, emotional experience full of joyous highs and painful lows for all concerned.

The debate surrounding embryonic stem cell research illustrates the moral and ethical pressure that the public brings to bear on the scientific community. However, while nonexperts often criticize scientists for not considering the potential negative impact of their work, ironically the public's reaction against such discoveries can produce harmful results as well. For example, although the outcry against embryonic stem cell research in the United States has resulted in fewer embryos being destroyed, those with Parkinson's, such as actor Michael J. Fox, have argued that prohibiting the development of new stem cell lines ultimately will prevent a timely cure for the disease that is killing Fox and thousands of others.

Each book in the series contains several features that enhance its usefulness, including an in-depth introduction, an annotated table of contents, bibliographies for further research, a list of organizations to contact, and a thorough index. These elements—combined with the poignant voices of people touched by tragedy and triumph—make the Social Issues Firsthand series a valuable resource for research on today's topics of political discussion.

Introduction

The reasons people have for immigrating to the United States are as diverse as the cultures they leave behind. The happiest stories are told by immigrants who jump at the chance for a new life, who see a land brimming with possibilities. Other stories are told by immigrants who do not come with such eagerness. For example, some immigrants regret leaving their home but realize that they are no longer safe there. Others come intending to stay only temporarily, to earn money or get an education. Yet others come involuntarily, often children who are too young to see or appreciate the advantages that their parents see. Regardless of why they travel, and no matter how enthusiastic they are about their journey, immigrants are always to some degree surprised by what they find in the United States. America is typically a different place than they anticipated. Changing their expectations to match their observations is just the first step in adjusting to their new home.

Starting from Scratch

Whatever social or professional status an immigrant has in his or her homeland, it is likely to change drastically upon arrival in the United States. Family status is the first thing to disappear; immigrants lose their established place in a community because they leave most, if not all, of their relatives behind. They commonly must start anew and find their place in American communities without the help of family. More immediately significant is a change in economic status. Traveling is expensive, living in the United States is expensive, and immigrants often have very little money when they leave their homelands. Professional experience, such as business knowledge or specialized skills such as medicine, is not likely to help them find work comparable to the jobs they held in their native countries. Unfamiliarity with professional or even conversational English is just one obstacle in building a new career, and immigrants from non-Westernized nations may not have any experience that would enable them to easily find work in industrialized American society. The first several years of an immigrant's life in the United States can be a blur of long days of hard work for little compensation and almost no leisure time. As researchers Monika Stodolska and Konstantinos Alexandris state, recreation is understandably "quite low on the priority list of immigrants who struggle to adjust to the new environment, who often hold several low wage, but physically demanding jobs and who have hardly any free time available." [1]

On the other hand, a change in status is not necessarily unwelcome. Despite the challenges, many immigrants discover that they are immediately better off than they were in their homelands. Refugees from war-torn villages now live in apartments on streets free from military occupation, in towns where food is plentiful and the water is clean. Individuals once persecuted because of their race or religion may no longer be marginalized in their community and can pursue whatever interests or lifestyles they wish. Immigrant children are welcomed into an ethnically diverse school system, and higher education is available to all students who qualify academically. For many families immigration represents a permanent change for the better and the difficult, crazy years do finally come to an end.

A New Person

Immigration transforms more than an individual's external circumstances; it transforms his or her interior life, too. An immigrant quickly learns not only how to navigate a foreign society for basic necessities, but also to speak a new language, use a new system of currency, and understand the nuances and etiquette of a different culture. Immigrants often gain courage, flexibility, and a multicultural perspective that come from having to adapt to an extraordinary situation. Although not all immigrants are pleased with their new lives, they are all transformed by the experience.

Children and adults, however, find themselves transformed in different ways. Born and raised in one culture, an adult immigrant's ethnic and national sense of self is not necessarily threatened by immersion in a new society. Adult immigrants, to varying degrees, undergo the process of acculturation, or, as professor of education Eamonn Callan defines it, the ability to "function in another culture" without "displacing [a] prior cultural identity." [2] Child immigrants, on the other hand, have less of a personal tie to the country of their birth and are much more likely to identify with American culture. Indeed, the process of emigrating is easier for children in many ways: They have the chance to learn the language sooner, receive the education they need for a successful economic future, and spend time at school developing a social network that includes many native-born children and adults. Still, their lives can be as difficult as those of their parents, albeit in other ways.

Juggling Two Selves

Immigrant children brought to the United States with their families are caught between cultures. As pointed out by Siyon Rhee, a professor at California State University, Los Angeles, these children "are expected to value and maintain their heritage and, at the same time, to learn another language quickly and to adapt to the host society." [3] Adapting to the host society of the United States means that children must learn the traits of independence and self-sufficiency, as well as all the technological and modern elements that pervade American culture. They do not always appreciate the same social behaviors and values that their parents do. Exacerbating the situation is the reversal of roles that some families undergo. Both Firoozeh Dumas and Irina Reyn, authors of two of the articles in this book, found themselves in a position of authority over their parents because they had the ability to understand American culture and the means to explain its mysteries and inconsistencies. Immigrant children are in the delicate position of having to become experts and teach the family about all things American while simultaneously maintaining and respecting the traditions of the family's ethnic heritage—a conflict at best and a contradiction at worst.

New Americans

Perhaps the biggest change immigrants can make is to permanently adopt the United States as their home. Legal immigrants who have resided continuously in the United States for five or more years (three years if an immigrant is married to a citizen) are eligible to begin the process of officially changing their nationality by becoming naturalized American citizens. It is a choice that nearly half of all eligible immigrants made in 2002, according to the 2003 report *Trends in Naturalization*, written by Michael E. Fix, Jeffrey S. Passel, and Kenneth Sucher of the nonpartisan organization Urban Institute.

Becoming a citizen is one of the most important steps an immigrant can take toward a prosperous future in America. Eugenio Vargas, who works for the Central American Bank for Economic Integration in Honduras, used data from the U.S. Census Bureau to compare the incomes of immigrants to the United States to the incomes of native-born Americans. He discovered that, although "individuals who come from non-English-speaking, less developed countries" economically lag behind native-born Americans and English-speaking immigrants when they first arrive, these disparities "seem to disappear as the individual spends more time in the United States,"[4] and these immigrants are even likely to "catch up" to immigrants from the English-speaking countries of England, Canada, Ireland, Australia, and New Zealand.

As time passes, an immigrant's increasing facility with the English language enables him or her to earn higher wages, receive more education, and make friends and develop relationships with other immigrants and with the larger community. Eventually, immigrants create a network of social and professional connections that is as complex as the familial and community network they left behind. Ensconced once again in society, immigrants balance and combine the best of their homelands with what they have learned in the United States. Just when their lives seemed to have changed the most, they discover that they have found peace and stability after all and look forward to a bright and prosperous future for themselves and their descendents.

Notes

1. Monika Stodolska and Konstantinos Alexandris, "The Role of Recreational Sport in the Adaptation of First Generation Immigrants in the United States," *Journal of Leisure Research*, Summer 2004, p. 379.
2. Eamonn Callan, "The Ethics of Assimilation," *Ethics*, April 2005, p. 471.
3. Siyon Rhee, Janet Change, & Jessica Rhee, "Acculturation, Communication Patterns, and Self-Esteem Among Asian and Caucasian American Adolescents," *Adolescence*, Winter 2003, p. 749.
4. Eugenio Vargas, "The Influence of Country of Birth and Other Variables on the Earnings of Immigrants: The Case of the United States in 1999 (Ethnicity and Immigration)," *American Journal of Economics and Sociology*, April 2005, p. 579.

SOCIAL ISSUES
FIRSTHAND

CHAPTER 1

Finding a Place in a New Land

A Cuban Sails to Freedom in America

Mirta Ojito

Mirta Ojito was sixteen years old when she and her parents sailed from the island nation of Cuba to make a new life in the United States. Her parents had been trying to emigrate since 1961, shortly after Fidel Castro came to power and established a restrictive Communist government that made emigration a difficult process. In April 1980, Castro gave to any person who wished to leave Cuba permission to do so but only from the harbor town of Mariel. The Ojitos, like 124,000 other Cubans, opted to make the short ocean crossing to the United States. On October 31, 1980, Castro closed the port.

In the following selection, Mirta Ojito describes how she, her sister, and her mother traveled on an American boat, the Mañana, *as it towed her father and American uncle in their incapacitated companion boat,* Valley Chief, *to international waters. There, they were picked up by a rescue boat and brought to America. It was a difficult journey for Ojito, who was physically seasick, homesick for the country and friends she did not get the chance to say good-bye to, and worried that the boats would separate and she would never see her father again. The full story of Ojito's emigration is told in her memoir* Finding Mañana, *in which she recalls her childhood in Cuba, what happened in Cuba when Castro took power, and what her life was like after emigrating to the United States. Since coming to America, Ojito has graduated from college, become a successful news reporter, won the Pulitzer Prize for journalism, and taught at several universities.*

I had remained in the same position—straining my eyes to follow my uncle in the distance—for too long. My neck hurt, and I no longer believed I could will his prompt return just by keeping my eyes fixed on his white T-shirt. I rubbed the back of my neck in an automatic gesture. Wispy clouds moved swiftly in the otherwise clear sky, and a slight breeze offered a break from the midafternoon heat. I squinted in the light.

The thought of losing my uncle frightened me. He was the only link we had to the rest of our lives. If he disappeared, we would be forced to stay in Cuba. And legally we were no longer in Cuba. We couldn't just pick up our lives where we had left off. They would never take my sister and me back in school. My father would not have a job, and no one would ask my mother to make dresses anymore. People would be afraid to be seen with a family that had tried, but failed, to escape.

My uncle's deep voice yanked me out of the darkness of my thoughts.

He was speaking to a tanned and muscular sailor, standing next to him. They were surrounded by armed Cuban soldiers. The sailor spoke English with an accent I had never heard in any of the black-and-white MGM films broadcast on Cuban television every Saturday after midnight. Although I had taken English lessons in school since the eighth grade, I didn't understand a word he was saying. He spoke as if the syllables had melted in his mouth. His eyes twinkled in the light, and he smiled when he looked at us. The man had sailed his yacht, *Mañana*, to the port of Mariel in a humanitarian mission, my uncle explained, and now he had come to our rescue. Everyone in the boat moved closer to him. Here was an *americano* we could trust. The man began to give orders to the younger men who accompanied him. I sat on the hard cement surface of the docks. From below I noticed something peculiar about the man's left arm. It barely moved while he talked and gesticulated with his right arm. My eyes followed the curve of his muscles all the way to the shoulder, covered by a tight light–colored T–shirt. Where the skin should have met the arpit in a smooth curve, there was a bulge, a somewhat clunky connection to his torso. The arm was fake, I relalized, but so similar to his other arm that it was almost impossible to tell them apart. The nails were perfectly shaped, veins formed an expanding web underneath the rubbery "skin" of his hand, and the coloring of the rubber, extending from shoulder to hand, precisely mirrored his skin tone.

The crowd dispersed to give the sailors room to maneuver. When the one–armed man threw a thick rope from the docks to keep the *Valley Chief* from drifting, his fake arm got tangled and fell into the water. Everybody gasped. My mother fainted, her body hitting the cement with a thud.

A young man, a member of the American's crew, dove into the murky waters of the port and after a few seconds came out triumphantly holding the prosthetic arm over his head, like a soldier in a war movie trying to keep his rifle dry. The American simply took the arm, shook the water from it, and put it on. My mother came to. An explosion of applause followed. It was a sign, I thought, of good things to come.

Before Mariel, I had never traveled anywhere outside the country or even very far inside Cuba. My longest, most exciting journeys had always been bus trips to my parents' small–town birthplaces in Las Villas. We would always arrive in Rancho Veloz, our first destination, around midnight. My grandfather Juan would be sitting in his wheelchair, waiting for us, wearing pajamas, his face fresh and smooth from a recent shave and his thinning hair carefully combed around his shiny bald spot. His gnarled hands would hold me by the shoulders away from his body, away from the hug I was aching to give him, and he would always say the same thing: My, my, how you've grown! You are a little woman already!

Folds of skin hung from his once–powerful arms, and his legs, no longer responsive, were nothing but bones covered by skin, purple and glistening from years of circulation ailments that had finally caught up with him. But his hands were still strong, his deformed fingers leaving red marks on my arms, as he finally relented and let me crush my face aginst his concave chest.

Abuelo, Abuelo, Abuelo! Grandfather! I would babble, not quite sure of what else to say. We would then sit and talk about life in Havana. My grandfather, who had lived with us for months at a time before his still–undiagnosed disease had confined him to a wheelchair for the past two yers, would ask about old friends, about his barber, about the condition of certain gardens in the neighborhood from which we'd often stolen white roses, my dead grandmother's favorite flower.

When I was a small child, he had been my most tolerant and faithful playmate. He allowed me to stick him with my mother's sewing needles when I thought I wanted to be a doctor. He taught me to play checkers and performed magic tricks for my friends and me, insisting that his knowledge and strength derived from an invisible entity he called Caballo Blanco, White Horse, whose power only he could summon by clicking the fingers of his right hand.

During our yearly vacations in the country, I sat at the table well past bedtime, listening to my grandfather spin his tales as he sucked on his pipe. I hated leaving him at the end of the summer. I would wave to him from the windows of the train as it chugged along past his house, until I had run all the way to the last car and there were no more windows to wave from, always fearful that I would never get to see him again.

And now I was certain I would never see him again. Tears ran down my face for the first time since I'd left my home, as I followed my mother to the *americano's* boat.

I jumped over the railing and stood on the bow of the *Mañana*. The name was fitting, I thought. Without looking back to the *Valley Chief*, where my father had stayed with my uncle, I made my way below deck, where a woman named Blanca was asking for volunteers to help her make sandwiches. I wanted to keep busy, but my hands were shaking. First the mustard, Blanca gently guided me, then the ham and the cheese. I followed her orders automatically, not daring to imagine what was going on up above, where I knew the captain would soon begin steering us out of the harbor.

It was hot in this improvised kitchen. Beads of sweat ran from Blanca's face to her neck, collecting in a giant expanding stain on her pink cotton blouse. I heard the captain begin shouting orders, and felt the boat seperating from the *Valley Chief* with a thud. Blanca handed me two more pieces of white bread, perfectly sliced as if no human hands had ever touched it. I thought of the fifteen–cent bread I stood in line for every other day: hard and coarse, uneven, clearly the work of a man and an oven, a communion of experience and fire.

I heard the sounds of the harbor: the Cuban officers barking orders through bullhorns, the thick lines of the sailboats— *ting-ling, ting-ling*—as they hit the masts, the waves lapping up against the sides of the *Mañana* with a deafening *whoosh, whoosh*. The sounds seemed distant now. We were pulling away.

A tear fell on my hands, and Blanca urged me to go up and give a good, last look to my land. You'll regret it later if you don't, she said sternly. I dropped the bread and the mustard, the ham and the cheese, and raced up the wooden stairs toward the bow of the ship, where I could see that the sun had begun to touch the waters of the harbor.

My heart was pushing against my throat as if it wanted to stay behind. I swallowed hard. I had always thought that I would leave Cuba during the day, when I could see my island in all its splendor just as I'd seen it on maps countless times: flat and green, with shimmering rivers crisscrossing its underbelly, bookended by mountain ranges, tall and regal like sentinels in the Caribbean that protected it from hurricanes and invaders and other perils of geography and history. Instead I concentrated on the contours of the land before darkness engulfed my scant view of the shores: patches of green, a flag flapping in the wind, a building on top of a hill.

Concentrate, I ordered my brain, urging it to record every small detail of my island. This is the last time I'll see Cuba. Take it in. Take it all in. I was momentarily distracted by the call of a bird before it dove into the water for its dinner, a silverfish, its scales sparkling with the last rays of the dying sun. I looked back to the land, but it had become more yellow than brown, the water more blue than green. I should have brought a rock with me, a little water, a handful of dirt, I thought, and stared hard at the horizon until my eyeballs began to hurt and the tenuous line of the shore melted into the horizon. Nothing but water now. I leaned over the bow and began to throw up.

None of my friends knew that I was leaving Cuba at this moment. I thought about Frank, still in Angola but due to come back any day now. I had not been able to tell him that I wouldn't be there when he retuned. In fact, very few people beyond our immediate neighbors even knew that we weren't home anymore.

My friend Kathy surely was the first person outside my block to learn that I had left Cuba. For years I had picked her up every day at twelve–thirty so we could walk to school together. If I was late, which was often, she would walk the two blocks from her house to mine and call my name from the street, knowing that her voice would carry through the always open terrace door. I bet she had done the same on Wednesday. I bet she looked up, saw the bare terrace, the closed door, and she knew. I bet she saw my neighbors' faces and they saw hers, and I bet no one dared say a word.

Perhaps not even the government knew that I was in this specific boat. I felt free for the first time in my life, and the feeling was unsettling. There was no longer any need to hide my family's desire to leave Cuba, since everyone who surrounded me was, quite literally, in the same boat. Yet I felt very alone, disconnected, as if someone had cut the umbilical cord that had kept me attached to my sense of self and place for sixteen years. I was no longer the top student vying for a spot in jounalism school. Nor was I the daughter of disaffected *gusanos*. I was nobody's friend or girlfriend. I was simply one more human being in a bobbing yacht heading north.

I had entered the world of exile, a zone where one must always walk alone, at one's own pace, and only after burying a part of one's soul.

I awoke with a violent stomach spasm, as if I were going to throw up, but my stomach was empty. I was totally disoriented. I didn't know where my head was or in what direction my feet were pointing. I wondered if someone had moved my bed. Then I realized I was not in my bed at all. I was on the cold, wet metal floor of the *Mañana*. I tried to stretch my arms and uncurl my legs, but I hit something soft. A person, perhaps? My sister was next to me, sleeping, though I saw that she, too, had been throwing up. Her long hair was matted with dried food. Someone was holding my ankle tightly. I sat up straight. A wave of dizziness overcame me, and I fell back, my head hitting the floor hard. My mother let go of my ankle and took my hands, caressing them. I could tell she was scared.

She was forty years old and alone with her daughters for the first time in her life. She didn't know how to swim, she'd never been in a boat, and she'd rarely ever been away from my father. What's wrong? my mother asked. I thought for a minute what to say. I was cold and hungry. I had an intense pain in my bladder because I hadn't gone to the bathroom for hours, perhaps a day—I'd forgotten. I couldn't feel my legs. My head hurt, as did my throat and stomach, from retching up bile. My clothes were dirty. My hair was matted. I hadn't changed or washed in almost five days. I felt like crying, but I was so dizzy that I couldn't even cry. And of course there was the pain of all pains: I had left Cuba.

Nothing, I told her, and closed my eyes again.

I had never been seriously ill in my life, not so that I was practically immobilized, as I felt now. In fact, except for occasional nosebleeds, I hadn't even been to a hospital. The last time my nose had hemorrhaged, just a few weeks earlier, I'd sat in the waiting area of the emergency room in the county's top children's hospital for six hours. To avoid the spectacle of my gushing nose, I had begun swallowing my blood. Finally, when I couldn't stand it anymore, I opened the door of the nurse's station and demanded to see a doctor. A nurse gave me some tissue to clean myself and gently told me that all the doctors were in a meeting of the Communist Party and that there was no one to see me until the next shift.

She led me to a bed and gave me a clean towel. There is nothing more I can do, *cariño*, she said, in the endearing way Cubans talk when they empathize but can't help you. Three hours later I was finally admitted. By then I had to be given shots to coagulate the blood and have the veins of my nose cauterized with electricity, which sent small, painful electrical shocks down my spine. I went home and seethed all weekend, convinced that even medicine had been contaminated by the politics that eventually choked everyone and everything around me.

My mother knew I was awake, though my eyes were closed. We've let go of the boat, she said, and I knew she meant that the *Mañana* had towed the *Valley Chief* to international waters, as arranged, and then let it go. I wondered where my father and my uncle were.

When? I asked.

Two hours ago, I think, she whispered.

Did you see them? Could you talk to them?

No, my mother said. I saw the lights in the distance.

What time is it?

She didn't know. I sat up with great difficulty and looked at her eyes, dark but dry. In the rush to leave Cuba, I hadn't even said good-bye to my father before we left the *Valley Chief*. I heard my uncle yelling after me to call his wife when we got to Key West [Florida], but I hadn't looked back. Darkness framed my mother's worried face and I felt the urge to touch her, to soothe her, but the effort of moving my head had been too much. I felt nauseated and lay back, trying to find a comfortable spot. A wave splashed us, and I tasted salt on my lips. It was Sunday, May 11, Mother's Day.

My mother was not going to get a card that day, I realized. I had mailed her one the day before we left our house. It was probably already under the door now.

Happy Mother's Day, I said just before the thick fog of seasickness enveloped me once more.

For as long as I could remember, I had lived with the fear that this was the year in which I would lose my mother. Ever since I'd learned that my grandmother had died at the age of forty, the day after my mother had turned sixteen, I'd dreaded that history would repeat itself, given the coincidence of our birthdays. My mother would be forty by the time I reached sixteen. She fueled my pessimistic rumblings by reminding me often that she was sure she would die young. One day, shortly before my sixteenth birthday, I'd awakened to the sound of her sobs. My mother, sitting next to my bed, was caressing my arms, my hands, my face. Frightened by the sight of her tears, I asked what was happening. Nothing, she said, but it will. And just like that, I began to live with the certainty that my mother wouldn't last me through the year.

She would be forty–one in October, and I was still sixteen. It was only May.

When I woke up again, the sun was hot on my sweaty skin, but I felt clammy and cold. People were rushing about, and I didn't know why. All my energy was concentrated on one immediate thought: I needed to get to a bathroom. My bladder was so full I couldn't move. I grabbed a roll of paper that my mother had given me earlier and carefully unzipped my pants. Under the navy blue blanket that covered me, I began to stuff the paper inside my underwear. I was sure I wasn't going to be able to get to the bathroom in time. My mother saw my distress and called for help. Two young men, the sailors who had helped the captain earlier, grabbed my arms and carried me to the bathroom, my useless feet dangling behind me. The men stood at the door, turning their backs to us, while my mother held me so I wouldn't fall from the toilet onto the dirty floor. Where was my father now?

In the summers, when we traveled to Las Villas, my father made sure to befriend the bus driver because he knew I would get sick on the trip and need frequent bathroom breaks. I often developed bouts of diarrhea or, worse, motion sickness while traveling. The buses lacked restrooms, so my father would search out the window for a bushy area, where even a large man like him could hide for a couple of minutes. Driver, can you stop for a moment? We have an emergency here, he would yell after taking a look at my pallid face. The driver would oblige.

For those inevitable moments, my mother carried a plastic bag full of colorful scraps of cloth, remnants of the dresses and pantsuits she sewed for her clients. Toilet paper was scarce. While I crouched on the fields, I focused on the intricate patterns of the scraps in the bag, trying to match each with the faces of my mother's clients. I knew that anything green and bold was usually Anita's, a young divorced woman who entertained my mother with stories of her torrid love affairs. Anything plaid or black and white belonged to the two fat sisters who always dusted their feet with talcum. Invariably, they left a chalky white trail on our floors whenever they came for a fitting. My mother would carefully pin the dress around their rolls of fat as I sat cross–legged on the bed and took notes of the alterations she needed to make.

I would walk back to the bus knowing that my father waited for me on the steps. He would tap my head softly as I, embarrassed but relieved, made my way to our seats, closed my eyes, and rested on his lap until the next needle–sharp ache pierced my stomach, bolting me awake.

I heard loud voices and running feet above deck as I left the tiny bathroom of the *Mañana*. We had arrived, it seemed. The sailors dragged me upstairs, where men dressed in military fatigues and carrying an olive green stretcher awaited. They fussed over me and, gesturing, indicated that I needed to be taken to a hospital. My mother refused, shaking her head forcefully, since she knew that the men didn't understand Spanish.

Pull yourself together, she whispered in my ear. I can't let them separate us.

Slowly I got onto my feet, and as I did, I began to hear familiar loud cheers of *¡Viva Cuba libre!* Men and women stood behind a wire fence shouting "Long live Cuba!" until they were hoarse. Another group sang the Cuban national anthem in an endless loop. Yet others hurled slogans aimed at Fidel Castro: *¡Abajo Fidel!* Death to the tyrant! I wanted to cry. This is why I had left Cuba, I thought, so that I would never again have to hear another slogan, so that I would never have to hear another death wish against a political leader. I turned my face from the crowd and followed my mother, slowly, very slowly, to the end of a line that snaked around a two-story, sun-bleached white building. There was a mat on the floor in front of a door with a word printed on it in English: WELCOME. I studied each letter but couldn't come up with the meaning of the word.

The queasiness disappeared as I took my first steps in the United States, shuffling behind my mother and sister in the line. By the time we had reached the front, we were each holding a piece of paper bearing our name and the name of the boat that had brought us. Hold on to this. It's very important, a man in a crisp uniform said. I held mine in my closed fist as I prepared to board a bus.

Just then a kind woman approached the line and offered to make phone calls for anyone who needed to get in touch with relatives. In the day and night we'd spent on the *Valley Chief*, I had memorized my uncle's home phone number and address. I wrote it on a piece of paper she handed me and wrote my aunt's name on top, drawing a circle around it, to make it stand out amid the myriad other numbers the woman had already taken. The doors closed and the bus rumbled off, leaving the old wooden docks behind.

In a panic I realized that I'd just spent my first moments in the United States and yet I had no sense of where I'd been. I ran to the end of the bus and looked out but didn't see a name or a sign, only the bright green rear end of what looked like a small ice cream truck pushing through the crowd of Cubans at the fence. Two scraggly palm trees framed a squat building at the end of the docks. A woman frantically waved a small paper Cuban flag. This must be Key West, I thought, and went back to my seat. . . .

The blurry images of Key West framed by the windows of the speeding bus confused me, and I wished that my father was there to explain it all to me. This couldn't possibly be the United States. Where were the tall, gleaming buildings? All I could see were old wooden houses, painted white or faded pastel colors, a thirsty dog sleeping in the shade of a screened porch, roosters crossing the streets as if this whole town were somebody's unkempt backyard. For a few minutes, the bus followed what looked like a toy train winding its way through short, narrow streets. When the little train turned and we passed it on the right, men and women with pink cheeks and white hats pointed their cameras at us. I suddenly became aware of what I must look like: My clothes reeked of vomit, my red-and-white checkered blouse had held up pretty well, but my red polyester pants were a shade darker than I remembered them. I would have given anything for a shower. I hadn't seen myself in a mirror for five days.

The bus stopped in front of a building that looked like a huge warehouse. Inside, the floor was lined with row after row of green army cots. Large windows, at least three stories high, let the light stream in like spotlights in a huge stadium. Crisscrossing iron beams formed random polygons in the high ceiling, and men in uniform—green, beige, white, navy blue—seemed to be everywhere. Long rectangular tables on two sides held sandwiches, soda, and gum.

I need to go to the bathroom, I said, and there was a metallic taste in my throat. My voice sounded hoarse, far away. It was the first time I had spoken to my mother and sister since our arrival.

On my way to one of the yellow portable toilets, someone called my name. I turned to see a blond woman with blue eyes and delicate features waving frantically at me, hoping to catch my attention. At first I thought she had confused me with someone else, and I smiled at her and raised my shoulders in a gesture of helplessness, but the woman insisted, and I began to walk toward her.

Halfway there, I realized who she was: one of my high-school literature professors, whom I'd known to be a die-hard revolutionary, the last person I ever imagined I would see in the United States. She had always been highly critical of people like my parents who did not support the regime. I turned and quickly walked away. The bathroom would have to wait. I could feel a blush spreading over my face and neck as I reached the cot where my family awaited. I was embarrassed that I had left Cuba and someone had caught me in the act. Never mind that she, too, had left. I felt like a traitor. Exactly whom I was betraying I didn't know. I covered my face so no one would notice I was burning with shame.

We huddled on one cot and waited for instructions and for a sign that my father and uncle were alive. At about 8:00 P.M., I heard my name called through a bullhorn. The name was somewhat distorted by the way the man pronounced it and by the echo of the bullhorn, but I was sure someone was calling me, and I ran toward the voice, my mother and sister following. Before we saw her, we could hear her voice: my uncle's wife, Tere. There they are! They are here! She was yelling to no one in particular. And then there we were, jumping with joy along with her and hugging her in relief.

She urged us to leave with a brother-in-law who had driven her to Key West, while she stayed with Olimpia, one of the aunts who had visited us in Cuba the year before, and waited for her husband and my father. In the rush to leave, she kept our new documents, the flimsy pieces of paper with our names on them, which she said identified us as Mariel refugees. We were upset to leave without my father and uncle, but my aunt assured us there was nothing we could do. Go home and rest, she said as she gently guided us to a shiny moss green car right outside. The driver was Bartolo, the husband of my father's older sister and also my mother's second cousin, a man I'd never seen before. My mother sat in the front with him, while my sister and I stretched out in the back and immediately fell asleep, shivering from the extremely cold air-conditioning but too shy to ask Bartolo to turn it off.

I woke up startled by the beam of a flashlight on my face. A policeman at the car's window was talking to my mother's cousin in English. Without the identification papers we had left with Tere, we couldn't leave the Keys, he said. We got off the highway and pulled into the parking lot of a large roadside restaurant, which, my mother's cousin told us, purported to have "the world's best Key lime pie." I didn't know what a Key lime pie was and had to ask him to explain. Thinking of food—limes, pies, cream, cakes—I fell asleep, certain that in a few hours somebody would wake me up with the food that I had always dreamed would be plentiful in America: a warm ham–and–cheese sandwich, with the cheese melting and the borders of the ham curling up from the heat of the toaster, accompanied by a tall glass of orange juice. I couldn't remember the last time I'd had anything to eat.

Sometime later I heard the back door of the car open, and I felt a warmth enveloping my sister and me. A large, familiar hand caressed my face, and I opened my eyes to see my father hovering over me like a giant genie from a magic lamp. I leaped at his neck and remained there for a long time, hanging on to the anchor we'd all been missing for a day and a half.

For about six hours after the *Mañana* had left them behind, my father and the others on the *Valley Chief* had watched the boat slowly take in water. No one despaired, though, not even the disturbed men the government had packed in the boat. My father said he was worried about us, but not for his own safety. He was sure Americans would rescue them.

At around 7:00 A.M., two Coast Guard cutters approached the *Valley Chief*, squeezing it from each side with their pneumatic fenders. Pieces of old wood flew everywhere, and for a few minutes it seemed as if what was left of the boat would sink before everyone had been rescued. But the *Valley Chief* held on. The cutters took the men aboard a U.S. Navy amphibious–assault ship, the USS *Saipan*. The ship was so huge—almost a thousand feet long, my father calculated—that when he stood on deck the sea seemed a distant presence, hardly threatening. In its bowels the ship kept seventeen helicopters. Dozens of refugees from other rescue missions were already on board. All were checked by doctors and received a warm but spicy meal of rice and beans and meat. Sometime in the evening, my father, my uncle, and the others were placed on helicopters and flown to Key West, where they found my uncle's wife and drove off with her until they noticed our car parked in front of the restaurant that sold the world's best Key lime pie.

With the first rays of the sun on May 12, we arrived at my uncle's house, in a city called Hialeah. Accustomed to seeing photographs of my relatives in New York, I found Hialeah a surprise and a disappointment, just as Key West had been. There were no tall buildings, no interesting architecture, no statues, bridges, or wide avenues, no sense of a city, really. And of course there was no snow. Outside the house, pretty with colorful gardens, it was unbearably hot. Inside, it was chilly, the hum of the air–conditioning following us from room to room as we examined our surroundings carefully, not daring to touch anything.

The ceiling sparkled, and the floors were slippery. Delicate porcelain figurines filled every table and shelf. Crystal lamps with tear–shaped pendants hovered over the living room, while thick, velvety drapes kept the sun out. The polished wooden table quickly filled with breakfast ham–and–cheese sandwiches and orange juice poured out of a plastic jug, not squeezed from oranges. I drank three glasses and asked for more. My uncle happily obliged.

I took a long bath that left a ring of grime around the spotless white tub. A cousin I'd never met before came by and gave me her old, scratched sunglasses, but they fit perfectly, and I was glad. Another took me to a store, where she said we could look, but not buy. My uncles's wife bought me leather sandals, and someone else cut my hair. I pleaded for a copy of *The Catcher in the Rye*, and within hours I had one, except it was in English. It didn't matter, for I knew most of it by heart.

A picture of our family was taken in the yard, standing in front of flowering gardenias that, oddly, had no scent. I was assigned to my youngest cousin's bed, in a room decorated with sports memorabilia and lots of shiny golden trophies. That night, when I finally lay down to sleep on sheets printed with elongated orange balls and brown helmets, an irrational thought kept me awake: how to return to Cuba on the same boatlift that had just brought me to the United States.

A couple of days later, we went to a makeshift immigration office near Hialeah to register our presence in the United States. A nurse drew our blood and took chest X-rays. As we waited for the results, we were called to a long table for an interview. A bald man with a military bearing but dressed as a civilian was in charge of my file. In flawless Spanish he asked my name. Before I could tell him, though, he said I could choose any name I wanted. It didn't have to be my real name.

You are in America now, he said. You can forget the past and begin anew.

I thought the man was joking, but his face remained serious, waiting for my response.

Thank you, I said, but I'll keep my name.

I didn't tell him that my name was all I had. My name and my memories.

Escape from a Vietnamese Prison

Thuc Nguyen

Thuc Nguyen and his brother lived in Vietnam with their aunt when they decided to flee the country rather than be drafted into the Communist Vietnamese army. Nguyen had already been jailed once for trying to leave the country; he did not want to be jailed again for refusing to be a Vietnamese soldier. In 1982, with the help of his aunt, Nguyen and his brother traveled by boat down a river to the ocean, where they embarked on another boat that took them out to sea. After a treacherous week at sea, they were picked up by a commercial oil rigger and brought to a Malaysian refugee camp. In 1985, they were sponsored by a cousin and traveled to his home in Danbury, Connecticut. Although he was already nineteen, Nguyen enrolled in high school and moved to New York. He now works as a deliveryman for a small business but finds true happiness leading a Vietnamese choir in a church.

Before I went into hiding, I lived with my aunt in the country in the south. We lived on a farm that grew crops of wheat. . . . When both my parents died in 1972, my aunt took in my brother and me. . . .

When my brother and I were older teens, this aunt helped us flee, although she did not want us to leave Vietnam, but we had to. It was very terrible there. Once before, I tried to leave the country, and for that I was put in jail for one year. I had tried to escape from prison several times.

Eventually, I made my last escape.

In jail, we are kept in a group of twelve people, and the police watched us all the time. If you go just about five min-

Thuc Nguyen, *The Chosen Shore: Stories of Immigrants*. Berkeley: University of California Press, 2004. Copyright © 2004 by The Regents of the University of California. Reproduced by permission.

utes in the jungle, there is no way they can find you, no way to search. Our job was to trample the trees. And I tried to look at whether the police were unaware of us, then I ran.

After ten minutes, they knew I was not there, and they opened fire, and I ducked. But in ten minutes, there was no way they could arrest me. The forest has many trees. When anyone escapes, they report the person's name to the city, which is about two hundred miles away. They reported my escape to the city of Saigon, but I lived very far from there, so the information never got back to where I was hiding.

My brother at that time was at home. He also had run away from jail.

Leaving Vietnam

Like every young man who has reached the age of eighteen, I had to take a physical exam and enroll in the army. The government required this law. Anyone who did not follow the law or refused to register was put in jail. I would have been caught if I refused the draft registration. I swear I'd rather be a prisoner than become a draftsman under the Vietnamese Communist regime.

[At] that time, 1982, I was forced to leave my family and move to a farm for temporary hiding. While I was staying at the farm with a country family, my brother had found the sole way to save me: to escape the country by a boat. Once the time had been scheduled, I left my homeland without hesitation.

On the way to the harbor, we encountered too much difficulty. We had to cross in the muddy fields and slippery banks. Some of us even slipped in the mud. After an hour, we reached the harbor. However, the boat had not shown up. We had to wait for it by moving back to the forest nearby the river. We moved because most police were patrolling the riverside. In the forest, we were miserable from mosquitoes. We had endured the cold and rain. The night was dark and full of fear. We waited until two in the morning.

One man with a black uniform appeared in front of us. "Let's go. Follow me," he said to us in a serious, whispered voice. We were all rushing after him. About fifteen minutes later, we all stood in a flimsy boat. This boat was about fourteen meters long and five meters wide. We were eighty-four people in the boat. We did not feel comfortable in the small boat. We could only sit where we were and could not move a bit.

The captain came up to the cabin and opened the cover of the hole. "Don't talk while we're traveling on the river," he said, then checked the cover. He did this because the police might be patrolling.

Six Days at Sea

After five hours we reached the sea. Crazy waves began splashing onto the boat. We all fell to one side of the boat. For thirty minutes, the boat moved up and down violently. Most of us began feeling dizzy and seasick and started to vomit. After twelve hours, we could only see the tiny shape of the homeland. For three days on the ocean, we only saw the sky and the water. We went on for five more days.

I don't think we slept on the boat. Maybe we slept when we were so tired, just one hour or two hours, but we had to wake again because on the ocean no one can have good sleep. We just sat and did not move. For meals, we had dried food. Most people were fleeing the country for political reasons, but some of them wanted to make a better livelihood elsewhere.

Our boat had only enough fuel for one more day. The captain was busy checking a map to find our destination. Water and food were running out. The heavy wind sometimes pushed our boat the wrong direction. The boat might have sunk into the Pacific Ocean if it ran out of fuel.

Again the heavy wind came. Everybody was in a panic and screaming riotously. "Stop, stop screaming. The boat will sink if you go on yelling," the captain shouted, "Don't be afraid, people."

My heart was speeding faster and faster. I thought we would sink in just a few minutes because there was a terrible hurricane. It made us so afraid that nobody could feel hungry or thirsty. But fortunately, the hurricane calmed down an hour later. Everyone thanked God it was over.

The engine was stopping gradually because it was over-heated. The captain stopped the boat temporarily to cool off the engine. We took a rest for two hours and then continued our journey.

End of a Dangerous Journey

Many people were worried and scared about how many more days the journey would take. Our lives would be in danger. I felt sorry and feared for us. Looking at the ocean, I imagined that the sea was a monster. It opened its mouth and waited to take our lives.

Surprisingly, we saw a tiny smoke line on the horizon.

"Oil driller. We've got it," the captain cried out. He assured us of this because he had experienced it in the navy. He steered the wheel straight to the destination. Everybody in the boat felt happy. The pressure of fear had blown out of their minds. Finally, it took six more hours to reach the oil driller.

The Malaysian navy saved us all. They brought us to the Pulau Bidong Island refugee camp just a few hours later. Thank God, we all survived. Our journey took six days in the ocean. . . .

From a Refugee Camp to Connecticut

Most of the Malaysians at the camp were police. There were no civilians. Most of the police were cruel because the people who lived in the island didn't have enough food for themselves. They wanted to have all the food on the island. If there was a coconut tree, and someone from the camp climbed very high to pick the coconut, the police caught this person. The police would bring him to the taskforce office and cut and beat him. The haircut punishment where they shaved off the hair was not so bad, but the beatings were. They even had a punishment where you had to serve them for one week in the office.

The food we received at camp was sent from many other countries. I was in the camp two and a half years. We had to live very simply. Life on that island was very difficult. Because we had relatives in the United States, we wrote a letter to them, and they helped us by sending money. But for many people they did not have anyone in another country, and they had to suffer terribly.

We had to go to school three days a week to learn English. We also had to do public work. . . . Many of the newcomers had to do the sanitation for the long houses. When the United States government accepted us, we moved from the island. My cousin from Connecticut sponsored us.

[In] the year 1985, I came to the United States with my older brother and lived in the house with my cousin, Ben, in Danbury, Connecticut. It was quiet and as peaceful as the countryside. . . . Everything was strange to me, but it also became the most interesting time I ever had.

A Bosnian Teen Starts High School

Anela

Anela was born in Bosnia, but when she was six years old, war forced her family to leave Bosnia and emigrate to Croatia. When the war drew to a close seven years later, Anela's family returned to Bosnia and its collapsing economy. Her father, once a college professor, left for America to seek better opportunities. There, he found work as a painter. In April of 2001, when Anela was fifteen, her father finally got the papers that enabled him to bring the family to live with him in Illinois. Anela—who spoke very little English—immediately started high school as a freshman. In the following article, Anela tells of starting her new life in America.

I was eleven years old when my father decided to move to America to seek a better opportunity for his family. My father left Bosnia for America.

He lived with my uncle. The reason my father emigrated from Bosnia was because of the economic situation. There was a lot of unemployment so it was difficult to survive and the only solution was to move to America. My father used to be a professor in Bosnia, but when he came here he worked as a painter.

After four years without seeing my father, he came to visit us. Although we were in touch with him, it was an incredible feeling when I saw him again. That same year he sent papers for us and we were on our way to America. I thought of America as an enormous, rich, powerful, stable economic country, after everything my father had told me. I was very excited to come here.

Anela (from Lyons Township High School in IL), "Fighting on My Own to the End," *NextSTEP Magazine*. Reproduced by permission.

It was really hard to say good-bye to my mother country and my friends, but I thought of my father from whom I did not want to be separated from and of better opportunity for my education and life here in America. I was fifteen years old when I came to America on April 9, 2001.

Starting High School Is Difficult

I went through a lot of tough situations and experiences, but my parents supported me, which gave me a lot of confidence to move on and to overcome every obstacle. The first day of school in my freshman year, at Morton East High School in Cicero, was indescribable.

When I entered to my first period class, all those strange faces were staring at me as if I came from another planet. I felt uncomfortable. I did not know anyone in school. I did not go to lunch on the first day. I sat on the stairs and I cried until the bell rang and I went to my next class in tears. I was experiencing the same horrible feelings that I once felt upon my return to Bosnia.

It was the worst experience I ever had. As a teenager, it is hard to start a new life in [a] different part of the world. When you are younger it is easier to learn English and easier to get involved with other kids. As a teenager, you want to try to explore what is outside of the world, new experiences, meeting and spending time with friends and having fun.

The Language Barrier

I felt like I did not belong here, because I did not know anyone. I wanted to go back to Bosnia where I left my friends and my family. Another issue that I had to struggle with was English. When I came here I knew a little English but that still was not enough.

Whatever I said, others had a hard time understanding me and I did not understand them either. When I was in Bosnia I was an excellent student and coming here and having difficulty learning tore me apart. Since I did not understand students I thought they were making fun of me.

I would come home every day after school and cry but I knew that crying would not help me. I survived war in Bosnia; English cannot be that difficult. The only class that was easy for me was math class, because the operations and numbers are the same as in Bosnia and I could understood it with [the] little English I knew. What surprised me was that students here are allowed to use calculators for their math class, while in Bosnia we could not, which made it easier for me.

Learning English Fast

My English teacher told me that the more I speak English the more I will learn it, so I did not care if students understood me or if they would make fun of my accent—I just wanted to learn English quickly as possible. I had confidence in myself and I knew I could do it. I would study for long hours at night and wrote English as much as I could in my notebook.

I would fall asleep with my English dictionary in my hands. I was tired but I did not give up. Now that I communicate with others and learn more about American culture, I see a better future for me here. As time passes I meet new friends that have something in common with me. Remembering everything I went through when I came here made me more determined and aware of life and my future.

A Bright Future

I am happy that people can understand who I am and I can understand them too. I have to take advantage of all opportunities available to me. My birthplace is still in my heart and will always be. Finally, after sixteen years of my life, emigrating from one country to another, I made it to America, the land of opportunity.

My parents left their parents and their land to come here for a better future and to have our dreams come true. I am fortunate to have opportunities that many people around the world do not have.

I am so grateful to my parents who gave me a chance to come here and so that I can achieve my goals.

An Ethiopian Boy Makes Friends and Enemies at School

Mawi Asgedom

Mawi Asgedom was a boy when he and his family—father, mother, two sisters, and a brother—left war-torn Ethiopia. They spent seven years living in a one-room hut in a refugee camp in neighboring Sudan and then emigrated to the United States. Their first American home was a motel room. When a church decided to sponsor them, they were able to move into a two-story house with a yard.

In the following excerpt from his autobiography, Asgedom tells of how he and his siblings adjusted to school life in America. The firm belief of his parents, that the United States offered plenty of opportunities to students who worked hard, inspired him to become a success. Asgedom eventually graduated from Harvard University in 1999. His story has been featured in many magazine and newspaper articles, and he has even appeared on the Oprah Winfrey *show. He now works as a motivational speaker for schools and corporations, addressing the topics of inspiration, respect, achievement, and leadership.*

From our very first days in America, my mother and father hammered into our minds the importance of excelling in school.

"Right now, we are among the poorest in the land. Neither your mother nor I will find good work because we lack schooling. We will have to work back-breaking jobs, we will never fully understand our rights, and others will take advantage of us.

"But if you, our children, work hard at school and finish the university, maybe someday you can help yourselves and help your family, too."

Mawi Asgedom, *Of Beetles and Angels: A True Story of the American Dream.* Chicago, IL: Megadee Books, 2001. Reproduced by permission of the author.

My parents may not have known much about this country, but they knew that the university cost more money than they had.

Making the Most of Opportunity

They had a solution, though. They told us that if we were among the best students in the land, we could earn scholarships and attend the university for free—in spite of our race and background.

"You are poor and black and we cannot buy you the resources that other parents can. But if you have enough desire to outwork all the other students and you never give up, you will win the race one day."

What's both beautiful and scary about young children is that they will believe most anything that their parents tell them. If our parents had told us that black refugees growing up on welfare in an affluent white community couldn't excel, we probably would have believed them.

But they told us that we could do anything if we worked hard and treated others with respect. And we believed them.

Unwelcome at School

Sometimes, though, faith was not enough. No one taught us that lesson quite like our classmates at Longfellow Elementary School.

They had never seen anything like us, with our thick, perfectly combed afros, our perfectly mismatched clothing, and our spanking-new XJ-900s, bought from Payless Shoe Source for under $7 a pair.

My brother Tewolde and I patrolled the same playground for the hour-long lunch recess. Kindergarten met for just a half-day, so my sister Mehret went home before recess.

Most of our classmates treated us nicely, others ignored us, and the rest—well, we could only wish that they would ignore us. We may not have understood their words, but we always understood the meaning behind their laughter.

"African Boodie Scratcher! Scratch that Boodie!"

"Black Donkey! You're so ugly!"

"Why don't you go back to Africa where you came from?"

We were just two, and they were often many. But they had grown up in a wealthy American suburb, and we had grown up in a Sudanese refugee camp. We were accustomed to fighting almost daily, using sticks, stones, wood chips, and whatever else we could get our hands on.

So it was usually no contest, especially when the two of us double-teamed them, as we had done so many times in Sudan.

Fending for Himself

Sometimes, though, our classmates found us alone. One time, a brown-haired, overweight third grader named Sam cornered me along the north fence of the playground.

All about the school, kids played soccer, kickball, and four-square. We had but one supervisor to monitor the hundreds.

I don't remember what I had done to infuriate Sam; maybe it was something that Tewolde had done, and I was going to pay for it. Whatever the answer, Sam wanted to teach me a lesson.

He bellowed at me, getting louder with every word, until his face blossomed red. He bumped me against the fence and gripped the railing with his thick, chunky hands, sandwiching me in between.

I pushed against him desperately and tried to wiggle out, but he kept squeezing harder and harder, until the metal fence began to tear into my back, leaving me unable to breathe.

I searched for the supervisor but could not spot her. Nor could I see my brother. Fearing that Sam meant to squeeze all the life out of me, I started to cry for help. He squeezed even harder.

Fighting Together

I think one of my brother's friends must have told him that Sam was suffocating me, because through the tears, I saw Tewolde exploding toward us. He came charging from the other side of the playground with all the fury of an angry bull.

Tewolde was half of Sam's size but he showed no hesitation. Without slowing, Tewolde leaped up, cocked his hand back and smashed it against the side of Sam's thick head.

Sam slumped to the asphalt and started to cry. But my brother had only started. He clenched his teeth and pounced on Sam's outstretched body, battering his face with punch after punch until Sam started to bleed.

I saw the supervisor coming toward our side of the playground, so I grabbed Tewolde and pulled him off. "Come on! *Nahanigh*, Tewolde! We have to go! Come on, before the supervisor sees us!" . . .

Making War with Other Africans

Tewolde and I even had confrontations with the only other Africans at our school: big, puffy-cheeked Frank and small, silent Mbago, a pair of brothers from Nigeria.

Both were in second grade with me, even though Frank was three years older than the rest of our class. How could that be?

None of us knew for sure, but we knew that he wasn't too bright. He used to pay other second graders to do simple math problems for him—five minus three, eight minus four, six plus seven—all for two cents a problem.

Even though we were from different countries, we still should have been brothers, defending and helping each other. But like our brothers in Africa, we were making war when we should have been making peace.

I tried to avoid them by playing on the opposite side of the playground.

But Mbago always provoked me. I think that he disliked me because I was poor and looked it, and he was ashamed to be African with me. When Frank was there, I had no choice but to let Mbago call me any names that he wanted. But whenever I found Mbago alone, and Mbago said anything mean to me, I always pounced on him and made him cry.

Invariably, he would return with Frank. They would corner me far away from the supervisor, when I least expected it, and beat on me until I had escaped or they had had enough.

Enemies or Neighbors?

They lived just down the street from us, less than one block away, so one day my bro and I hid in some bushes and waited for them with long, lean sticks in our hands. We would show them, Sudanese-style.

We sprang on them. *Slash. Scream. Slash.* They ran desperately.

But we were faster and cut them off. And Tewolde let out his anger. "Don't you ever touch my little brother again or you'll get it even worse!"

We strutted back home, victorious, even laughing as we recounted the incident.

But then we thought of whom they might tell, and our laughter stopped in a hurry. We retreated into our house, afraid of what we had done.

When we heard the frenzied knocking on our door, we knew that our time was up.

Their parents stood outside, guarding bruised and teary-eyed children. My parents yelled out in anger for us to appear. "Did you do this? Don't you dare lie or I will make you lost right this moment!"

Lifting us by our ears, my parents screamed at us and threatened us until the Nigerian parents had been appeased. Then the parents began talking about Africa, immigration, and all of the things they had in common.

"Would you like some *injera*? How about something to drink? That's all you are going to eat? How about some tea? Please. Visit us anytime you want. Of course not! Do not call first. You know that our people do not believe in appointments; come over whenever you want!"

It was the start of a beautiful friendship.

CHAPTER 2

Adapting to the American Way of Life

An Indian Man Is Partially "Americanized"

Jay Vithalani

Although he was born and raised in Bombay, India, Jay Vithalani grew up speaking English as his first language, watching American programs on television, and listening to American music. He believed himself already "Americanized" when he moved to Boston in 1991 to start college. However, as Vithalani writes in the following narrative, he still surprised every day by some element of American culture. Vithalani currently attends the University of Iowa in the Nonfiction Writing Program. This essay won first place in a contest sponsored by the university.

From 1991 to 1998, I lived in Massachusetts, first as an undergraduate in a small college town and later as a graduate student in Boston. My education and upbringing in Bombay, too, were of a peculiarly "Western" kind. English is my first language. . . . I went to a school which used, until the eighth grade, only American textbooks. I grew up watching American TV shows and listening to American popular music. [Artist] Jackson Pollock and [singer] Joni Mitchell are not "alien" to me; neither are [essayist Ralph Waldo] Emerson and the Emmy Awards. In that sense, I have not really experienced "the shock of the new"—sometimes exhilarating, sometimes terrifying, sometimes just comically baffling—in my recent move from Bombay to Iowa.

No overwhelming culture shock, a sufficient number of movie references to throw out during . . . conversations . . . , a fondness for macaroni and cheese dinners—why, then, am I bothering to write . . . this essay at all? Because, despite all these protestations of being "Americanized," I have, practically

Jay Vithalani, "Coming to America," University of Iowa Office of International Students and Scholars, International Student Essay Contest, 2005. Reproduced by permission.

every day, some experience which reminds me that I *have*, after all, crossed oceans and cultures, and that the process of "adjustment" is not complete and perhaps never can be. Small though these quotidian reminders may seem, they are, to me, cumulatively significant and valuable.

The Midwest Culture

Iowa City is reassuringly similar to other college towns I've lived in. Nevertheless, this is my first time in the Midwest and at a Big 10 school. Walking down a relatively empty street, I often get a nod of acknowledgement or a "Howdy" from strangers; needless to say, this does not happen very often in Bombay or Boston. My first view of the Iowa plains, from the window of the tiny plane that brought me to the Eastern Iowa Airport, was also one of topographic strangeness. I said to myself, idiotically, "There are actual cornfields and grain towers! Not a highrise in sight!" I was prepared, in theory, for proverbial Midwestern warmth, for farms, for houses rather than gigantic residential monoliths; the actual experience of these was surprising nonetheless. . . .

Despite some valiant attempts, I have never been able to follow football or baseball. Their ubiquity in American culture—and particularly at a place like the University of Iowa, where the Saturday football games seem to absorb the passion of the entire population—is a constant reminder of my status as an "outsider," though admittedly not in a very wounding way. I have had two haircuts in Iowa City, at two different barbershops. Both places were festooned with signed football posters, and both barbers, almost automatically, asked me whether I'd seen the recent game. I sheepishly had to answer no. My knowledge of football is restricted to the fact that the Iowa quarterback is named Drew Tate and that we recently defeated Indiana 38 to 21. So much for cultural literacy.

Adapting to America

Then there is the matter of shopping and the relatively new development of mega-stores. When I first entered the Target store at the mall, I was simply overwhelmed by the immense size of the place and the mind-boggling number of *things* in it. And the experience was repeated when I went to Best Buy, Office Depot, HyVee. . . . After a lifetime of buying what I need at small or midsized local stores, the exposure to these giants was almost paralyzing at first: "Where do I start? It seems like I'm going to get lost!" Pretty soon, of course, one gets tolerably used to the bigness, and with the help of new friends I seem to have managed my shopping excursions mostly unscathed.

After two months, I still find myself heading over to the driver's side [of a car] (which is the passenger's side in India) when a friend picks me up. I still occasionally say "lift" rather than "elevator" or "footpath" rather than "sidewalk." I've [learned] many new words ("pine-sap," "snarky"), but the nuances of "nerd," "geek," and "dork" continue to elude me. I'm still wonderfully surprised by the superb public library and still a little disapproving of students who eat during class. I'm still getting used to living on my own (and my neighbor's constant banjo music). No one seems to have a snakecharmers-and-maharajas image [stereotypes about Indian people from films and stories] of India, which is great. And it's still fun to see the look of surprise on my new friends' faces when I tell them that Bombay's population is seven times that of all of Iowa.

Perpetually Perplexed by the Weather

Within all the large familiarities, constant and plentiful strangenesses, "gaps," revelations, and lessons seem to have been [my] burden. But there is one lesson I'm pretty sure I'll never learn, one constant American (and Midwestern) fact I'll never get used to: the unsettling changeability of the weather. One day it's 50 degrees, the next day it's 80. Lots of 90+ days in the summer, lots of subzero nights during winter. My tropical instincts, used to sameness in the weather and minor seasonal variations, rebel against the "illogicality" of this. Well, I have t-shirts and shorts as well as sweaters and gloves. One can't learn everything, and perhaps a daily reminder of this particular strangeness isn't after all a bad thing, [but rather] an antidote to a kind of complacency. And so it is that I end every day, in my un-Americanness, with a quintessentially American ritual: listening to what the next day's weather is going to be like.

From Chinese Woman to American Wife

Hong Xia Wang

Hong Xia Wang became Mrs. Hong Devitt when she married an American man. She was living in Shenzhen, China—a warm city near Hong Kong—when she was granted a spousal visa on April 12, 2005. One week later, she and her husband flew from Hong Kong, to Tokyo, to Seattle, and then to Billings, Montana. Devitt was surprised to see snow on the ground, but weather was only the first of many differences she found between Shenzhen and American life. In the following article, Devitt describes how she adjusted to the changes.

My name is Hong Xia Wang. I came to America April 19, 2005, from China. I am also known as Hong Devitt because I am married to Stephen Devitt.

The city I came from is Shenzhen. It is close to Hong Kong. My husband traveled to China to accompany me to the U.S. consulate in Guangzhou [a Chinese city] where I was interviewed by visa officers. I was given a K3 (spousal) visa[1] on April 12.

My husband and I packed our things and began our journey [to the state of Montana]. I had to leave many things behind I am still waiting for. Among them were my warmest clothes because my husband told me, "Montana is warm now." He was wrong.

A Very Long Journey

We traveled from Shenzhen to Hong Kong by ferry. This was the hardest part of our journey because we had many large

1. A spousal visa permits a noncitizen to come to America to live with a citizen husband or wife.

Hong Xia Wang, "Her First Fourth," *The Billings Outpost*, vol. 8, June 30, 2005, p. 1. Reproduced by permission.

bags to carry. We finally got to a Hong Kong hotel that had bus service to the airport. We had a nice dinner there, and my husband told me that when we got on the airplane, I would be leaving the Chinese language behind. He was right.

We flew to Tokyo and then to Seattle. . . . When we landed there was snow on the ground. I had not been in snow for 14 years, since I left Wuhan [a city in China she used to live in] to move to Shenzhen in 1991. Shenzhen is a very hot city.

In the airplane from Seattle, I looked down upon many mountains, and I was a little afraid. "Where is Montana?" I thought. "Where are all the people?" My husband's mother met us at the airport, and my husband drove her car down into Billings [Montana]. It was the first time I had ever seen him drive a car.

Differences Are Everywhere

Everything in Billings was different from Shenzhen. There were no traffic jams here. The houses were all short. There were not many tall buildings, and the food was all different.

On my third night, I became very ill with a high fever because of the cold weather and I had a very bad headache. My husband had to take me to the hospital in the middle of the night. It was very different from a Chinese hospital. For one thing, I was in a room by myself. Another difference was the amount of paper. In China, you get a little book the doctor writes in. Here, they gave me paper from a computer when we arrived, while we were in the room and when we left. The biggest difference was the cost. My husband asked me how much this would cost in China (getting an IV with medicine). I told him about 100 RMB [Renminbi, Chinese currency] (about $12). Here it cost about $1,000.

As I got a little better, my husband took me to see many stores in Billings. These were also very different. There were many clothes for fat people. I think maybe American food and the lack of exercise (most Americans have a car so they do not walk) make people get fat.

In restaurants in Billings, I tasted sugar in many things. They served fewer vegetables and too much meat. I told my husband not to order me tea in Billings restaurants because they do not make good tea here. I always liked to drink green tea in China. I miss the morning tea (a breakfast meal) served in many Shenzhen restaurants. They serve many dishes that are not available here. Shenzhen's restaurants and grocery stores always had live fish and seafood in tanks. Fresh seafood is very good for health, and does not make people fat. . . .

Meeting Friendly People

Another big difference is that people in Billings are much friendlier than in Shenzhen. In Shenzhen, people do not talk to waitresses (there is also no "tipping" in China) or store clerks. In fact, people do not talk to people they do not know. In Billings, everybody talks to everybody and people help each other.

For example, one day I went downtown without my husband. I was going to the Social Security office to ask about my card and number. In China, I worked all the time since I was 18—first as a nurse in the army and then as a meteorologist in the Wuhan and then Shenzhen airport. My husband had filled out the paperwork to adjust my status to permanent and to get permission to work. My husband had to go to work every day, so I went to ask myself and I got lost. A very kind couple helped me. They called my mother-in-law and gave me directions so I could get home. I was very thankful for them.

Getting lost is very easy for me because in Shenzhen I always took the bus or taxi, both of which are very cheap. A bus ride costs between 2 and 5 RMB (25 to 75 cents), and a short taxi ride is about 12 RMB ($1.50). My husband pointed out a Billings bus to me, and there was no one on it. Much of the time in Shenzhen, you have [to] stand on the bus, but I know where all the bus stops are in Shenzhen.

America Is Full of Trade-Offs

The gyms in Shenzhen are more expensive than in Billings, and the gyms here are much better. You get to swim for free; there are better machines and fewer people in the gym. Many times in Shenzhen, I had to wait for machines. But in Shenzhen there were dance-based aerobics classes which I enjoyed.

Before I came here, my workmates talked to each other about America. They had never visited America, but they got information about America from magazines, the Internet, TV, and movies. In their minds, America is very beautiful: many rich people and there was the ability to get rich in America. So I dreamed of a beautiful America.

I really enjoyed my job in Shenzhen. I worked in the meteorology office at the Shenzhen Airport, and did this work since 1988. I studied meteorology at the university at Nanjing. I would like to do that kind of work in the United States, but I do not know how to get this job.

I saw a New York City photograph and I thought it was beautiful with big buildings. Billings doesn't have many tall buildings, but the people here are more friendly and kind than in the big cities, so I like it here.

A Mongolian Makes Many Choices in America

Dulmaa Enkhchuluun

In 2000 Dulmaa Enkhchuluun, or "Enkee" to his friends, came to America from Mongolia to pursue a Bachelor's degree. While at college, Enkee had his first real taste of American culture. In the following selection, he describes the vast number of choices available to Americans. Put off by the excess and waste of American consumer culture, Enkee promises to remain true to his Mongolian cultural beliefs.

I am a 26-year-old Mongolian male, and everyone calls me Enkee. My full name is Dulmaa Enkhchuluun. Under the Mongolian system, we only have one name, but my mother's name is Dulmaa and out of honor to her, I use her name as my first name or what you would call my family name. She gave me the personal name Enkhchuluun, which comes from two Mongolian words, *enkh* meaning peace and *chuluun* meaning stone. She hoped that in a world of great uncertainty I would be as strong as stone but also as peaceful as a stone.

Five years ago in 2000, I came to Minnesota to pursue my BA degree. It was my first trip abroad, and I had no idea how the American academic system functioned or even how Americans lived. I knew that the images I saw on television and in films did not represent real life in America but I had no idea what to expect aside from those images. I thought of America as a large, powerful country associated with democracy and, of course, Hollywood. My English was not good enough to enroll in regular classes; I had to take English as [a] second language course for six months at St. Thomas University before enrolling as a full-time student at Augsburg College.

A Confusion of Choices

My introduction to American life came through the college experience. Within only a few days I was delighted, overwhelmed, and even horrified. I was delighted by the great choice of food. On campus and within a few blocks, I could find pizzas, hamburgers, French fries, and the drink machines allowed me to have as much pop, milk, or tea as I wanted. Just walking into the cafeteria gave me more choices in food than I was accustomed to making in a whole year back in Mongolia.

Yet, the choices were also baffling at times. I could not understand the difference in choosing between a college and a university. Why were St. Thomas and Hamline universities while Macalester and Augsburg were colleges? Within each school there were so many choices. Within my own sphere of interest, what could possibly be the difference in programs of International Studies, International Relations, or Global Studies?

Choosing Wastefulness

My introduction to American life came at many levels, and when I met my first American roommate I saw the horrible side of choice and freedom. I came to America with one small suitcase. I kept everything that I had in it. Each piece of clothing was folded exactly as my mother taught me. My pen, pencil, and notebook were each carefully wrapped, and I treasured them. By contrast, my roommate had a roomful of stuff. He owned more books than a library, yet he never seemed to read. He had enough music CDs for a music store, but he played the same one over and over at an incredibly high volume. He had more electronic equipment than my whole school had in Mongolia. He piled clean and dirty clothes in the closet, on the floor, under the bed, and on the desk, yet he wore the same shirt and jeans every day. Although we had a great variety of food in the cafeteria, he filled the room with the bags of chips, sodas, and boxes of leftover pizza and dried sandwiches.

Satisfied with Enough

In five years in America, he was the sloppiest and crudest person I ever met, and at times I felt like leaving and going home. Yet, now that I look back, I can see that it was an important experience meeting him. I learned about the value of choice and the abuse of choice. Knowing him and seeing how he lived made it clear in my mind that I had to choose carefully what I wanted from America. I had to select those things that could help my family and country, and I had to avoid the excess. Having choice was worthless unless I could use the choices wisely. I learned from him that I would never have more food than I could eat, that I could never have more equipment than I could use, and that I would buy only what I needed. I also made a promise to myself to remain as hard as a rock and as peaceful as a rock in America. In order to remain hard, I would walk or ride [a] bike . . . even in the coldest weather.

In five years I learned to be an American in some parts of my life and even in some parts of my heart, and yet I strove to remain a Mongol and to be my mother's son. I wanted to return home to Mongolia with the best education and training that America had to offer, but I wanted to be the hard and peaceful man that mother intended me to be. After all, in giving me the name Enkhchuluun, she gave me my destiny and my character. I wanted to live up to her hopes for me.

SOCIAL ISSUES
FIRSTHAND

CHAPTER 3

Caught Between Cultures

No Longer Russian Enough, Not Quite American

Irina Reyn

The child of Russian Jews marginalized by Soviet society, Irina Reyn and her parents immigrated to the United States in 1981 when she was in first grade. She discovered at an early age that a fluent command of English gave her power in her new school and country. Reyn went on to work in a variety of fields that required strong language skills, from writing and publishing to theatrical stage managing to the news media. In the following selection, she writes that she still struggles with her cultural identity, feeling neither completely at home in America nor totally part of the Russian community. She views herself in stark contrast to her firmly American younger sister, who was born in the United States and has never lived anywhere else.

Since my arrival in America, acquiring outsider status has always been easy. A couple of weeks ago, I was visiting my former Russian literature professor at Rutgers University. Three other Russian girls were waiting for him outside his office. While waiting, they entered into a conversation, during which they realized that they were all recent immigrants. They were speaking in Russian. Eventually the topic turned to "Americanized" Russians. It was obvious from their dismissive tone that the girls had contempt for these "Americanized" Russians. "They think they're so cool because they came when they were ten or eleven," one scoffed. "Yeah, but they're not Russians. Not really," another replied. "They refuse to speak Russian and only hang out with Americans." "But," the first chimed in, "they will never be Americans no matter how hard they try." The girls quickly looked over at me.

Irina Reyn, *Becoming American: Personal Essays by First Generation Immigrant Women*. New York: Hyperion, 2000. Copyright © 2000 Meri Nana-Ama Danquah. Reproduced by permission of the author.

I knew then that standing apart from the group—this particular one or any other—would be a theme that would play itself out for the rest of my life. If those three girls represented my Russian culture, I was definitely not a part of it. They intimately knew a country I have not stepped foot in since I was seven. Recognition of this fact brought about a familiar mixture of anger and envy. It seemed as if their identity had been fully established, while mine may never truly be. . . .

Memories of a Russian Childhood

Having so few scraps of memory from my first seven years in Russia, I try to will myself to remember important moments. It is as though by fleshing out those pictures in my mind, I am shaping them into a foundation solid enough to hold up my identity as a Russian-American. I most fear forgetting the details of my childhood. Without them I will never really know myself. The images that flick through my mind are brief random snatches of time—mushroom hunting in the woods, nightmares of the witch Baba Yaga, burning-hot miniature milk bottles lining my back as a treatment for a cold—but none are as vivid as my first day of school. On the evening of August 31, I went to bed feverishly. The following day was one I had heard about from parents and grandparents, from *Spokoinii noche, malishi* (Good night, children), the one television show I watched from 8:30 to 9:00 P.M. every night. It was a day talked about in hushed whispers with my friends in kindergarten, and fictionalized in books I could read as well as ones read to me. . . .

I still remember tossing in my bed until I saw hints of daylight edging through my lace curtain and finally resigning myself to the excitement of the day. . . . Patiently sitting in my wooden chair, I waited for my parents to awake and enter the door to my room, sweeping me up in the chaos of the day. Having no camera at home, I was taken to a professional photographer to commemorate the day. . . .

A Communist Initiation

No other first day of school—not my first day of third grade in Brooklyn, my first day of junior high in Queens, or my first day of high school in New Jersey—would ever feel the same to me, have the same sense of rightness. I was a child at home in the world, in the place that made sense and belonged to me. I was supported in all my actions not only by my parents and peers but by the communist state, which at every step was always there, urging me on proudly, telling me that what I was doing was perfect, exactly the way it should be done. In November of that year, I was an *Octabryonok*, something I knew was to be treated with pride, not only because I was wearing the white pinafore, but also something to do with the formal nature of the occasion: the principal's voice during the rally that day, the poster of Lenin [a founder of communism and the first premier of the Soviet Union] pointing his finger at me, the accentuation of the authoritative horn above all other instruments. Only later would I discover that I was taking part in an initiation ceremony enfolding me into the communist state. . . .

I was flushed with triumph and the knowledge that I was enveloped in a community. What I didn't know . . . was that at that moment my parents were already making all the necessary plans for our move to the United States, to New York. After being on a two-year waiting list, they, along with thousands of other Russian Jews, were finally allowed to leave. . . .

Bringing the Russian to America

I bid farewell to my friends from Moscow and my Ukrainian summer dacha [country house] in a daze, half-listening to my mother's promises that America would have boxes of fifty crayons and dolls with long hair and extensive wardrobes. Growing up in a provincial Ukrainian village, my mother always dreamed about crayons herself, turning over in her mind the smooth surfaces of things she would reinvent. Putting me to sleep on the few nights before we left, she regaled me with fictional descriptions of the sparkly new place we were going to, then played an English lesson on my record player. "Apple, *yabloko*," I would hear a man's deep voice say before anxiously drifting into an uncomfortable sleep. "Apple, *yabloko*."

Our first apartment was in Flatbush, Brooklyn, in a one-bedroom which I shared with my parents. . . . Our apartment was a confused fusion of the old and the new—*Charlie's Angels* and the Smurfs melded with my Russian records, Judy Blume slowly eclipsed Pushkin, Blondie and Madonna drowned out Alla Pugacheva. My parents were all too happy to let the transformation take place—it would allow me to slip painlessly and naturally into this new culture. . . .

During the first year in school I frantically tried to hide the fact that I could not speak English. In the first month of third grade I took to doodling instead of writing, passionately believing there was a possibility my teacher would not realize my essay "What I Did Last Summer" had suddenly become a series of interlocking ovals in my able hand. Despite my parents' concern that I would never speak English fluently, by the end of my first year, in third grade, I had already won the spelling bee. That did not stop the kids from calling me "commie" [communist] every chance they got.

Upon first hearing this slur, I was perplexed at its meaning, and asking my parents produced no answers because they were equally confused. Apart from technological competition with the U.S., my parents were not taught to hate the Americans. So I had nobody to explain this heady insult that would not completely disappear until college, mostly because the children themselves did not know the meaning of their own words. It was only during glasnost and the Gorbachev[1] period that people around me became aware of the need to shift their thoughts and language. Over the years my defini-

---

1. Mikhail Gorbachev, the General Secretary of the Communist Party in the Soviet Union, implemented glasnost, a policy of public and government openness that greatly increased freedom of speech.

tion has evolved for Americans around me. Since my childhood corresponded with the end of the Cold War, I was at first viewed with suspicion by other children, in high school with dismissal, and in college with fascination in my assimilated otherness.

Fitting In

I enjoyed school, especially English class, but never understood American children's loyalties and friendships, which seemed to me to be arbitrary and ephemeral. I was awed by their command of space, but sensed that once claimed, the space was not to be shared. I was not able to formulate the impression that American children are raised with a certain degree of confidence, independence, and self-reliance, that the degree to which relationships are needed seemed to be alleviated due to their ability to maneuver smoothly in their environment. Being born of a collective country, Russians' friendships take on the covenant of family and the relationships tend to be full of earnest ardor and vehement devotion.

Not surprisingly, my shyness and intensity drove people away and I tended to gravitate to other immigrants like myself, who felt the same displacement. Yet at the same time, I believed that English was empowerment and studied it worshipfully. I sensed the power of language in classes and on the playgrounds. . . .

In America, people clamor for belonging and acceptance, but it seems so much simpler to remain jagged and edgy. A duality exists within me that permeates every aspect of my life. My Russianness wants so badly to be like everyone else, but as an American I am proud of an insight into another world that I somehow have a claim on. This split divides me until everything in my life is defined by its relation to its opposite. Yet I can never say I am a citizen of both countries. That is the uniqueness of the Russian-American experience. Russian Jews left with a bittersweet taste in their mouths, something I may have been too young to experience, but the residue of which was always visible in the adult conversations. . . .

It is with these contradictory feelings that I view a return to Russia in the near future. I know I need to go there to understand fully myself, but I am so afraid to be disappointed by the place, by the people. But what makes me most frightened about going back is the prospect of feeling no warmth there, no home, as though the country would wearily and dismissively say to me, "Why did you come here? Go back to America. There is no essence of you here." I fear that when I visit childhood friends and relatives, we will sit across a wooden table and they will see only a plumed, foreign creature eyeing them wildly.

I know I cannot return to my country of birth idealistically thinking I will be enveloped in its history, greeted as one of its own. Being a severely economically depressed country, there is no indulgence for humoring my nostalgia. I am often advised not to interact too intimately with Russians when I visit for fear that I would be viewed with envy and bitterness for my comfortable lifestyle. Apart from the "New Russians" who greatly profited from the recent capitalistic surge, most Russians are barely scraping by. Being pragmatic by necessity, my relatives would not understand my not working in a practical vocation like engineering or computer programming, but instead living single in Manhattan, with no prospect of a family of my own before me, a self-indulgent writer. I know how lucky I am to have the luxury of commodious analysis without the personal suffering.

New York is teeming with Russian immigrants, and I always overhear snippets of conversation on the subway, in the Century 21 department store, in the produce section of the supermarket. My instinct is to join the conversation, invite myself over for dinner as though they are all my relatives. "I'll bring cognac, take off my shoes," I imagine telling them in explanation of such a seemingly rude self-invitation. "I'm Irina." (For no doubt someone in their family has the same name.) I am half-surprised they don't know me or acknowledge my relation to them. . . .

Becoming Something New

Russians gather to be among their own people, but the longer they are in this country the more removed they are from Russia itself. It is the closest thing I have to a residual instinct, though, being there among my family friends and relatives who have formed a group of their own—neither Americans nor Russians—but the émigré circle, who speak with authority about a country that is changing without them. And so the country doesn't belong to me, doesn't want me, and I struggle with that knowledge along with a residual fear that I am American now and all pretensions to another culture are just that.

However, if I want to know what I would be like had I been born in America, I need only to look at my eight-year-old sister. Leading a fully American suburban existence in New Jersey, she has never needed to dream of fifty crayons. She has two rooms in the house, every Disney video, and dozens of computer games. She goes to school with the same friends, has sleepovers, and goes trick-or-treating every Halloween. She slips easily between worlds, proudly singing the lyrics to the newest Backstreet Boys song, while at the same time knowing how to use Russian to bring about a pizza delivery. She is a child who knows her own power, shrugging when complimented, quick to display her sharp memory. . . . I envy the ease with which she navigates her world, her insouciant reaction to her environment, her confidence about her place in it.

I was home this past September when she got out of bed to face her first day of third grade. She languidly got up, brushed her teeth, scanned her closet for a suitable outfit. She finally picked out navy blue Guess? sweatpants and a deep red Guess? sweatshirt with the words "Guess? For Girls" emblazoned on it. Then she patiently waited for my mother to brush her long brown hair and ran downstairs for a bowl of Cap'n Crunch and milk. Grabbing a Lunchables (with pepperoni pizza and a Rice Krispies treat), she grabbed her electric blue JanSport backpack and hopped out the door waving to her friends in the silver car in our driveway. I look out the window affectionately at the girl that could have been me—but wasn't.

A Nicaraguan Immigrant Longs to Return to Her Homeland

Yamileth

Yamileth is an undocumented Nicaraguan immigrant who traveled to America in 1988 to earn money to send back home for her peasant family. In the following selection, she describes her experience in the United States, first working in Oregon as a housekeeper for a couple named Penny and Mark and then searching for a better-paying job in Los Angeles. Although she appreciates how working and living in the United States has benefited her and her son, she dreams constantly of returning home.

Penny and Mark knew I was a Nicaraguan without papers. I told them that if they still wanted to hire me, I'd do the best job possible in whatever they told me to do. I took the job because I had to work, but I was afraid, more afraid of the language than the job. What I didn't know, I'd learn, but the language? It was the first time that we were going to have contact with people who spoke only English. Mark spoke just a little Spanish and really tried hard to communicate with us, but, as it turned out, language wasn't really a problem. From what I could understand, we were the first Nicaraguans with whom they had talked. They wanted to know more about our country. It was nice that they felt moved in our presence.

They showed me the house, and, with a lot of patience, how to work the washer and dryer. They showed me the room where we'd sleep. It was the first place I've worked where I've had my own room and my own bathroom, and carpeting everywhere. I decided that I'd definitely like working here!

Adjusting to a New Life

The first day, I had to learn everything. I was afraid of using the dishwasher, so for two days, I washed everything by hand. I didn't make much food because I didn't know what to cook. I told them to explain everything to me so that I could get things ready for them. In my country, we don't make large fancy meals—we weren't able to buy much—so, more than anything, I knew how to make beans, rice, and maybe some meat. Little by little they understood me and taught me.

The first few days were the hardest because Penny and Mark went on vacation in Mexico and left us alone. We had been there so little time and I didn't know if robbers might try to break in. I felt responsible for everything. I said to myself, "If someone breaks in to steal things, maybe the police won't believe me and instead they might think we're the robbers and that we sold everything for money." So many things were in my head.

We had to be ready for anything. When a tree branch broke outside, we got tense. We didn't know who could be after us. Door-to-door salesmen scared me, so we wouldn't go to the door. We were also afraid of getting lost. We had only walked a couple of blocks from the house before the family left for Mexico. There was a little plaza, as they say in Lake Oswego [Oregon], where we bought sweets and little things to eat when we watched television in our room. We spent our time eating popcorn in front of the TV, and the next day we cleaned the house and ate popcorn again. That's how we lived, closed up in our room. They had given us a nice TV set to watch, so we left only to check the doors and the mail. Then we closed ourselves in the room again.

Penny and Mark returned from their vacation and things became easier. I was still afraid to cross the streets because they had told me you could get a ticket for doing that. We Latinos aren't used to having the law enforced. In the United States, if there's a law, you have to respect it. I'm not afraid of the ticket, but I am afraid of their discovering that I'm walking around without papers. I'm always afraid the authorities will catch me.

As time went on, I worried less because Penny and Mark always told me not to worry. If I had trouble, they'd said they'd assume financial responsibility, arrange my papers, and do whatever I wanted. But that really would have made me feel obligated to them since I often got the urge to return to my country. To have them do all that work—spending money and time arranging my papers—and then announce at the end of the week that I was leaving? So I didn't ever tell them that I'd stay. I had come with the idea of working and then returning. Be it good or bad, that was my idea.

Forming a Bond with My Employers

We all got along well and became fond of each other. I learned how to use the microwave and the vacuum. The house was small, so by noon I'd have the housework done, the clothes washed and folded, and then we worked in the yard. After Penny and Mark saw what we were doing, they bought roses and other plants. We made the yard beautiful. I never stopped working in the garden. We planted carrots, onions, lettuce. So pretty!

While I was using an ax once, I hurt my back and it ached for days. They knew I didn't feel good, but I didn't tell them why. It embarrassed me to have hurt myself when I knew how to use an ax and hadn't gotten much work done—we like to work hard in Nicaragua—and I thought I'd get myself fired.

I had no problems living with Penny and Mark. I told Penny to tell me when she didn't like something, and when I saw something I didn't like, I'd tell her. When it was necessary, the three of us—Mark, Penny, and I—would sit at the table and clear things up. It was a good life. They loved me a lot. . . .

[My son] Miguel and I slept on a small mattress on the floor because the hideabed made my kidneys hurt. One day, Penny found out and asked us why we slept there. We told her the hideabed was soft and said we slept on the floor one day and on the bed the next. But that wasn't true. Sometimes we messed up the bed just so she'd think we slept there, but we didn't. We always slept on the floor. Once she realized that, she went out and bought two beds, along with luxurious bedspreads. We had a closet for our clothes, several dressers, a television set, and a VCR, just like high-class people.

After Penny changed the room, Miguel came in as I lay there reading with my feet crossed. "Well, well, well, look at us!" Miguel said. "We should have a photograph taken! If they could only see us now in Nicaragua!" We made jokes, and he teased me by saying, "*Señora*, turn on the television set, please." The next morning I got up early to make breakfast. It wasn't my job to do that, but I thought it would help. That's how I paid back the wonderful way they treated us.

In Many Ways Still a Stranger

When they came home after work, I went to my room. In general, I like to be alone. I like my privacy. I like to listen to music and watch television. I like to talk with people, but I'm not a lover of being with a crowd. I say only what's necessary.

They liked to take us with them when they went out. Even though Penny and Mark don't have a lot of money, they belonged to a club where Miguel could swim. I didn't like to do that, though, so on my day off, Sunday, I stayed in my room and read. I hardly left the room. It embarrassed me to eat on Sunday because I felt I hadn't done anything. How could I eat if I hadn't worked? We bought tortilla chips and sodas for the room, and a creamy cheese to spread on bread, so I didn't have to leave the room to eat. I did this every week. I got some books from a library . . . and I'd spend the whole day reading. I didn't leave my room. I really didn't. They'd knock on the door and call, "Yamileth, don't you want to eat?" "No thank you," I'd tell them. I wouldn't leave until the next day, when they'd ask me, "Did you read the whole book?" I really liked being in that house. They loved my son, and they loved me, too. . . .

I celebrated the tenth anniversary of the triumph of the Nicaraguan Revolution, July 19, 1989, in Portland . . . and it made me sad. Not many Nicaraguans were there, but lots of North Americans and especially Mexicans. I saw a Nicaraguan flag and heard Nicaraguan songs. At that moment, I thought I'd never return to Nicaragua, I'd never again hear those songs there. I felt alone, and I started to feel a desperate need to be with my people. . . .

Trying to Make More Money in L.A.

[Yamileth's sister Leticia, who lived in Los Angeles, told her that a job was available that paid more money. If Yamileth earned more money, she could return to Nicaragua sooner. She decided to leave Oregon to pursue this opportunity.]

By the time Miguel and I returned to Los Angeles, Leticia and [her] girls had been living in their apartment . . . for several months. It's better and larger than the first one. There are two couches, both given to us by friends, and two small tables, one that came with the apartment and one that was given to us. There's one big bed, a small cot, and two mattresses. The kitchen is in the hall and is in bad shape, but the refrigerator is in the worst condition of all. There's a gas stove and a place to wash dishes. The carpeting is bad. Lots of cockroaches, rats, and mice. Miguel and I sleep on the floor, but they haven't bitten us. I've seen the rats, though, and when I get up for water at night, I see mice running around when I turn on the kitchen light.

I made the biggest mistake of my life when I left Oregon and came back here to Los Angeles. I believed that what Leticia told me was true, even though I know Leticia lies sometimes. I made the mistake of believing that she really had work for me. My head filled up with lies. What Leticia really wanted was for me to clean the house, like a maid, and to watch over her children. "What am I going to do in Los Angeles?" I asked her when I realized the truth. It was my biggest mistake. I've regretted leaving Oregon a thousand times. . . .

Leticia told me I'd make two hundred dollars a week in Los Angeles, and I'd soon have enough money to go to Nicaragua. I was desperate to return as soon as possible. I spent some of what I'd saved in Oregon to come to Los Angeles from Oregon, and here I waited, getting more anxious every day. Apparently, I had to wait for someone else to leave the job before I could have it! Just not knowing how things were in Nicaragua increased my panic. . . . Time passed, and I made no money. The job didn't materialize, either.

Regretful and Homesick

If I had stayed in Oregon, Miguel would have received a better education, learned English, and continued to advance. I wouldn't have the fear of gangs that I now have, and I'd have saved more money. I would have been able to send money to Nicaragua all along. I sent money home three times from Oregon; but from Los Angeles, only once the whole time.

Miguel said, "It'd embarrass me to go back to Penny and Mark after Leticia lied to you about the work you were going to have." He said we'd return defeated and in shame. He made me feel embarrassed about having been deceived by my own family, to have left something so good and to have come here for something so bad. I couldn't bear to show my face to Penny.

And when I realized that there was no job waiting for me in Los Angeles, I felt so alone, as if they were playing games with me. This was no laughing matter, not a game, not a joke. I don't play games with anybody, and I don't expect anyone to do so with me.

Penny called and asked if I wanted to go back to Oregon, and I said I would return. I talked with Miguel one night while we were sleeping on the floor. I asked him what he thought, and he said, "You said we were coming to Los Angeles to work and make more money, but we're doing nothing here. Instead, we have more problems than ever." I started to cry. I didn't want to return to Oregon because I didn't want to see them after I had dropped everything to find a better job—after everything there had been so good—and found no job at all. Things like that can't be forgiven.

I'd cry at night because I didn't have enough courage to tell Miguel, "Let's go to Oregon, little one. Let's go." I felt like the most disillusioned woman in the world. I wanted *la migra* [enforcers of immigration laws] to catch me, along with my son, and send me back to my country. Even Miguel, who doesn't think of consequences and lives only for the moment, said, "Let's go to the places where *la migra* catches people and let them find us. That way we could go back and not pay. We'd have nothing, no clothes, but we'd be in Nicaragua."

If I weren't going to Nicaragua . . . I'd ask Penny to forgive me. I don't know how I'd do it, but I'd go back to their family. They're good, very affectionate. I had no problems with them, and they had none with me. And I'd have Miguel go to school.

A Struggle to Remain Indian

Shoba Narayan

Shoba Narayan has lived in three countries: India, Singapore, and the United States. She has degrees from American universities in psychology, art, and journalism, and has published many articles in a variety of newspapers and magazines, from the New York Times *to* House Beautiful. *Her book,* Monsoon Diary, *was published in 2003. She currently lives in Bangalore, India. The following article first appeared on a Web site aimed at an audience of Indian people living in foreign countries. In it, Narayan explains that when she was a resident alien in the United States, she had conflicting desires to blend in with Americans and to display her Indian heritage.*

I am an immigrant. I straddle cultures, juggle identities, and carry labels. The INS [Immigration and Naturalization Services] calls me Resident-Alien, the IRS [Internal Revenue Service] calls me Permanent Resident, Americans call me Indian, Indians call me Non-Resident Indian, surveys call me Asian-American, and job applications ask if I have a Green Card.

I got my Green Card last year. The process took two years and cost about $5,000. I spent hours filling [out] forms that the INS routinely sent back asking for more documents, yet another birth certificate. A local police station took my fingerprints to check if I had a criminal record; a clinic designated by the INS gave me a complete physical, including an AIDS test and sent the results in a sealed envelope.

A grave-look[ing] immigration official in Hartford, [Connecticut] opened the envelope, asked me if I had ever been arrested, if I had worked illegally before stamping my passport. My Green Card, which, as it turned out, wasn't green, would follow.

Shoba Narayan, "Confessions of a Cross-Carrying Immigrant," *Rediff on the Net*, January 4, 2000. Reproduced by permission.

Like most immigrants, I came to America in search of opportunity. I was tired of India's caste prejudices and century-old traditions. My father had worked for 20 years before he could afford a car. I wanted a car, maybe even two. I wanted a home, to live the American dream. I wanted to go from rags to riches. And I didn't want to wait 20 years for all that to happen. Naturally, I came to America. The never-ending expanse of choices in this country fueled my ambitions, lifted my spirits.

Here, I could achieve anything, become anyone, except, perhaps, the President. The realization was exhilarating. What I also came to realize was that with every choice came a sacrifice. With every achievement, I was losing a little of my identity. Lifestyle choices that came so naturally to the folks back home became agonizing decisions for me. Should I stick to the Indian community in the U.S., or should I make American friends, knowing that I could never be one of them?

Should I wear the colorful Indian clothes that I love, or should I quit wearing them in public because I am tired of being stared at? Should I keep my hard-to-pronounce Hindu name, or should I Anglicize it, like many Chinese had done? Should I celebrate Christmas, a tradition that I didn't grow up with, or should I ask for a day off from work to celebrate Diwali, the most important Indian holiday?

Should I stay in this country, or should I go back home?

Every Indian dreams of going back home. The isolation that is part of the immigrant culture, combined with the stresses of being a foreigner, makes us nostalgic for the familiar sights, smells and sounds of home. America, however, seduces us with the promise of wealth and the "good life." Most of us succumb and stay put.

Every now and then, there are nasty incidents. Like the Dot Busters—a gang in New Jersey that identified Hindus by the dots on their foreheads and attacked them, and then attacked anyone who looked like an Indian. Like the svelte brunette in an exclusive Manhattan soiree, who drawled that the "immigrants had spoilt California" for her. Like the stranger I encountered one snowy night.

"Go back to where you came from," he hissed. Well, I felt like telling him, if each of us said that to each other, the United States would become empty. And it could also lose its sense of balance.

What immigrants—particularly from the East—have given the United States is a sense of balance. They bring Yin values to a very Yang culture.[1] They temper the swinging pendulum with spirituality, and bring it to a Buddhist Middle Path. Into a land of excess, they bring in values like contentment and letting go. To mix some metaphors, they keep the melting-pot from running over.

Another thing that immigrants offer is perspective. When people ask me about the starving children in India, I tell them about the paradoxes in this country. The media tells us that incest, rape, and other crimes against children are on the rise in the U.S. Yet, the very same people who abuse their children will wait politely in line for a schoolbus to pick up children! I find that hypocritical.

Fielding questions is part of being a foreigner: Where are you from? Why are you wearing a dot on your forehead? Does your name mean anything? Do people still ride on elephants in India? Who'll be your role model? The questions drum inside my head like Paul Simon's song in the album, *Graceland*. Sometimes I get so fed up that I make up the answers or lie outright. But then, when I meet an "exotic" person, I find myself asking the same questions. I suppose it is part of being human to make connections and establish roots.

What many people—including me—forget is that a person cannot represent an entire country. For a long time, my behavior at every instance was exemplary. I was always polite be-

1. In many Asian cultures, the Yin and Yang represent opposites that, when brought together, signify balance.

cause I didn't want Americans to think that Indians were an impolite race. I always delivered 120 percent because it would help another Indian get hired.

Routine acts became deliberations. Simple choices became political dilemmas. If a white person tips poorly, then he or she is just a poor tipper. If I do the same thing, I am a poor-tipping Indian. So, never mind the bad service, never mind the lousy food. I have to leave a good tip. Otherwise, the next Indian that eats here will automatically get lousy service, because the waiter will think that all Indians are poor tippers.

I am sure every minority has gone through the guessing and second-guessing that comes with being stereotyped. After a while, it gets to you. Being an ambassador for my country became too much of a burden. I began to resent it.

These days, I try to be myself—failings, rudeness, warts, and all. It is difficult because at some point, I know someone is going to watch me slurping my soup or doing something equally "rude" and think that all Indians don't know table manners.

My father—a poet and philosopher—once asked me why I had decided to live in the United States. I thought about it for a moment and said, "Dad, I want to be a writer. If my books sell to the American market, they will sell all over the world. Once I become a successful author here, I can move back to India and still be successful."

My dad smiled. "What if you become so successful that you forgot what you wanted to say?" he asked.

Confusion and loss are my crosses. I will have to bear them, even if I can go back home.

An Iranian Woman's Appearance Confuses American Onlookers

Firoozeh Dumas

Firoozeh Dumas moved from Iran to California when she was seven because her father, an engineer, was transferred there by his employer. Dumas graduated from the University of California at Berkeley in 1988. She is the first Middle Eastern woman to be nominated for the Thurber Prize for American Humor, for which she was a finalist. In the following selection, she describes how strangers and neighbors mistakenly assumed she and her family were from Mexico, Peru, or Alaska, and how they reacted when they learned she was Iranian.

In America, I have an "ethnic" face, a certain immigrant look that says, "I'm not Scandinavian." When I lived in Abadan [Iran] my mother and I stood out because we looked foreign. Abadan's desert climate, which resembles that of Palm Springs, produces olive-skinned inhabitants. My mother and I, because of her Turkish ancestry, possess a skin color that on [actress] Nicole Kidman is described as "porcelain" and on others as "fish-belly white." In Abadan, people always asked my mother whether she was European. "Well," she'd always gush, "my aunt lives in Germany."

When we moved to California, we no longer looked foreign. With its large Mexican population, Whittier could have passed as our hometown. As long as we didn't open our mouths, we looked as if we belonged. But just one of my mother's signature rambling sentences without a verb ("Shop so good very happy at Sears"), and our cover was blown. Inevitably, people would ask us where we were from, but our answer didn't really matter. One mention of our homeland and people would get that uncomfortable smile on their face that says, "How nice. Where the heck is that?"

What an Iranian Looks Like

In 1976, my father's new job took us to Newport Beach, a coastal town where everyone is blond and sails. There, we stood out like a bunch of Middle Eastern immigrants in a town where everyone is blond and sails. People rarely asked us where we were from, because in Newport Beach, the rule of thumb was "If not blond, then Mexican." People would ask me things like "Could you please tell Lupe that she doesn't have to clean our house next week, since we're going to be on vacation?"

One would think that the inhabitants of Newport Beach, a town two hours from the Mexican border, would speak at least a few words of Spanish. But in a place where one's tan is a legitimate topic of conversation ("Is that from last weekend at the beach?" "No, I got this playing tennis yesterday"), learning the language of the domestic help is not a priority.

During my first year in Newport Beach, my junior high was conducting mandatory scoliosis checks. All the sixth-graders were herded into the gym where we waited for the nurses to check the curvature in our backs. When it came my turn, the nurse took a long look at my face and said, "Oh my God! Are you Alaskan?"

"No, I'm Iranian," I replied.

"No way!" she shrieked. "Bernice, doesn't this one look Alaskan?"

As Bernice waddled across the gym, I wanted to make her an offer. "How about I tell Lupe not to come next week since you're going to be on vacation, and we just call it a day?"

During that same year, I was asked to speak about my homeland to a seventh-grade class at my school. The girl who had asked me was a neighbor who needed some extra credit in social studies. I showed up complete with my books in Farsi, a doll depicting a villager weaving a Persian rug, several Persian miniatures, and some stuffed grape leaves, courtesy of my mother. I stood in front of the class and said, "Hello, my name is Firoozeh and I'm from Iran." Before I could say anything else, the teacher stood up and said, "Laura, you said she's from Peru!" . . .

So home I went with my Persian miniatures, my doll depicting a villager weaving a Persian rug, and my books. At least my mother didn't have to cook dinner that night, since the thirty grape leaves were enough for all of us.

An Unpopular Country

During our stay in Newport Beach, the Iranian Revolution took place and a group of Americans were taken hostage in the American embassy in Tehran. Overnight, Iranians living in America became, to say the least, very unpopular. For some reason, many Americans began to think that all Iranians, despite outward appearances to the contrary, could at any given moment get angry and take prisoners. People always asked us what we thought of the hostage situation. "It's awful," we always said. This reply was generally met with surprise. We were asked our opinion on the hostages so often that I started reminding people that they weren't in our garage. My mother solved the problem by claiming to be from Russia or "Torekey." Sometimes I'd just say, "Have you noticed how all the recent serial killers have been Americans? I won't hold it against you."

From Newport Beach, I moved to Berkeley, a town once described as the armpit of California. But Berkeley wasn't just any armpit, it was an armpit in need of a shave and a shower, an armpit full of well-read people who had not only heard of

Iran but knew something about it. In Berkeley, people were either thrilled or horrified to meet an Iranian. . . . Sometimes, mentioning that I was from Iran completely ended the conversation. I never knew why, but I assume some feared that I might really be yet another female terrorist masquerading as a history of art major at UC-Berkeley. My favorite category of question, however, assumed that all Iranians were really just one big family: "Do you know Ali Akbari in Cincinnati?" people would ask. "He's so nice."

Less Problematic Ethnicities

During my years at Berkeley, I met François, a Frenchman who later became my husband. It was during our friendship that I realized how unfair my life had truly been. Being French in America is like having your hand stamped with one of those passes that allows you to get into everything. All François has to do is mention his obviously French name and people find him intriguing. It is assumed that he's a sensitive, well-read intellectual, someone who, when not reciting [the French poet] Baudelaire, spends his days creating Impressionist paintings.

Every American seems to have a favorite France story. "It was the loveliest café and I can still taste the *tarte tatin!*" As far as I know, François had not made that *tarte tatin*, although people are more than happy to give him credit. "You know," I always add, "France has an ugly colonial past." But it doesn't matter. People see my husband and think of Gene Kelly dancing with Leslie Caron [movie stars from the 1940s]. People see me and think of hostages.

This is why, in my next life, I am applying to come back as a Swede. I assume that as a Swede, I will be a leggy blonde. Should God get things confused and send me back as a Swede trapped in the body of a Middle Eastern woman, I'll just pretend I'm French.

CHAPTER 4

America's Benefits

A Hmong Christian Puts Faith in Western Medicine

Zai Xiong

In 1975, a group of Laotian communists formed the Lao People's Democratic Republic and began the process of imprisoning and "reeducating" Lao citizens who had fought against them in the Laotian civil war. Many of these citizens were Hmong, a group of people who lived primarily in the mountains of Laos. Zai Xiong's family are Hmong, and when Xiong was an infant, his family fled their village and lived in the jungle for three years before finally relocating to the United States.

As a baby, Xiong suffered from a 50 percent hearing loss that his parents blamed on a bad spell or a spirit. Their attempts to treat it with a Hmong shaman in Laos were ineffective. Living in America at age sixteen, he reevaluated his role in the Hmong culture and decided to visit a Western doctor, who discovered that he had damaged eardrums from an untreated infection. Surgery restored his hearing to 85 percent. Against the wishes of his family, he converted to Christianity and is now a Mormon elder, but he still considers himself Hmong.

When I was about sixteen years old, there was one day I came home from high school, I came into my bedroom and sat down at my desk, and I am thinking about life. I guess I kept on hearing about people who are Christians but who are still in the Hmong culture. I heard about this Jesus that people are talking about, how he could restore people with hearing loss and all those things. I had a very bad hearing problem.

According to my parents, when I was a baby they took me down to a swamp and they lay me near some bushes. They

Ghia Xiong, with Lillian Faderman in *I Begin My Life All Over: The Hmong and the American Immigrant Experience*. Boston, MA: Beacon Press, 1998. Copyright © 1998 by Lillian Faderman. All rights reserved. Reproduced in North America by permission of Beacon Press. In the rest of the world by permission of the author.

said that after that I had a bad spell on me, because there was probably some bad spell where I was laying—or maybe it was a spirit's home and I had crushed it. There was a curse on me, on my hearing, that was brought to me by whatever spirit was there. They tried very hard to fix my ear. They called in the shaman to do a ritual many times. When they looked into my ear they couldn't see anything—only ear fluids that were coming out.

Finally, we came to America. And I kept thinking to myself, "Why, why do I have to be the only child that has to go through all this and not my brothers and sisters?" It really bothered me, especially when I became sixteen and boys and girls were talking together and could hear each other and could carry on a conversation fine.

A Chance to Hear Again

But one day about that time, when I was asking myself why I had to suffer like that, a missionary couple from the Church of Jesus Christ [of] Latter Day Saints came knocking on the door. They were telling me about this healing power and everything. I was really surprised by what they were saying, that I would be able to hear again.

They gave me things to study, and I found out how these things really work. Then I took missionary lessons and they taught me about the purpose of life, where I came from, why I am here, where I am going. They also taught me how I could get my hearing back. I studied everything very careful and I felt very peaceful, comfortable, quiet. . . .

I prayed a lot about getting my hearing back. I had 50 percent loss, and now after all my prayers I have 85 percent hearing. The answer I got from my prayers was that I needed to see a doctor. It was the prayer that gave me the strong feeling I could hear again. I learned, "After you pray, you do your best to help yourself and God will also help you." My best was to find a doctor to give me some tests, and he said he could do something to gain my hearing back. He found out that I didn't have my eardrum at all in both of my ears. That was why I couldn't hear. He said something got into my ears and I had an infection, and I never had any medication to heal it. He said he was going to use some small part of my skin to make an eardrum.

Afraid to Tell His Family

At first my mom didn't want me to do that. She was scared, and she said that it wouldn't work because they tried everything for the last fourteen years, and they always took me to a shaman. We were active in shamanism. My uncle—my dad's younger brother—is a shaman, and my father is a bamboo pipe player. He plays it very well, and I'm his son, and it was very hard for me to become a Christian. If I would not have had such a faith, such a trust and confidence in who I called upon, then it would be very hard for me to move out of the shaman religion and come into the Christians.

So I had two mixed feelings: One is about my family and relatives, about "What if they disown me? How would I handle that? How will I be living on with my own self in a world where there is so much confusion?"—and at the age of sixteen getting a job is hard. I was afraid of my family loss. But then I told myself, "I have such big faith, I have such great love and concern that I will be able to overcome this."

One afternoon I went to my mother. I had a feeling that I needed to go to her first. And I said, "You know Mother, I found this church that I have a lot of strong feeling about. And this church will be able to provide me with a lot of ideals and help me with healing of my hearing. I will be able to hear again, and then I will be able to hear all of you."

She was very concerned about me going to church. She said, "No, you're the only one who wants to do this. None of your relatives are going, and how can you go by yourself?"

And I said, "You know, Mom, I can handle this. This is America. And this is life in America. America is freedom, freedom of religions."

Hmong, Not Christian

And my mother said, "But you are still a Hmong. So it doesn't matter where you are, you are still going to be a Hmong. You're not going to church and be a Christian."

I felt hurt. I told her that nobody else could help me with my hearing. "You all have been trying for fourteen years and it hasn't been successful. Now I want to try something new, for me, for my life, and for my future."

After that she just sort of cried and became quiet because she could not answer me. Then she told my father and he said, "You crazy! Why are you doing this when none of your relatives are going?" He yelled at me. It was really bad. I didn't think it was going to be that bad.

He said a bunch of words in Hmong. He said such things like, if he was performing a shaman ritual, being his son I would have to be there. But if I become a Christian person, how will I help him? Why not stay with him and help him out?

Hmong *and* Christian

So for the first couple of months or so, I was just sneaky. I didn't have a car yet so I just called up the missionary people and told them to pick me up because I don't have a ride. I knew my parents weren't happy with me, but I was too big for them to spank me. And I felt I just had to go to the church meetings, I had to find out more about Jesus.

Once I used to look up to shamans as my spiritual leader. I looked up to them as my healer and I looked up to them as my guide. I guess they did their best to try to heal me, but it didn't work, so maybe it's not good for me. It might work for other people, but for me, no. So after I felt that shamanism wasn't successful for me, for my hearing, I shifted gears and found out about this new doctrine. I felt like, "I will go and find something that heals me, but I will not forget who I am. I will not forget that I am a Hmong."

I told my mother again, "You have tried your best, now I will try mine." So after I told my mom, I just went to the doctor and gave them permission to do whatever they needed to do to make me hear again. With my heart I felt that my prayer had been answered and that everything will be okay. After two hours of surgery, my brother came to pick me up. He shook when he saw all the bandages on my ear. Then after about a week I went back to the doctor and he removed all these bandages: Small sounds became big sounds for me! At sixteen I did all this by myself, because my prayer was answered.

A Mexican Immigrant Learns the Secret to Success

Javier Lares

Javier Lares first left Mexico in 1991 to become an undocu-mented worker in the United States. Although he worked hard, he found it difficult to get ahead in his job, in part because he did not speak English. Many years of thirteen-hour workdays, however, left him too tired to study a new language. Lares was deported to Mexico when a coworker reported him to the immi-gration authorities after an argument. A year later, Lares and his new wife returned to the United States. This time, he found a job that gave him time to enroll in classes and study English. As Lares states in the following narrative, his improved speaking and writing skills brought him more opportunities and more money to support his new family.

I am Javier Lares from Mexico. I am a man who tries to be better and better. I don't like staying in the same place. When people don't study, we have to work in different jobs where there is no progress. Trying to progress is really hard. Working in different jobs is hard when you cannot advance.

I remember twelve years ago when I left Mexico. Some people had come from Houston to Mexico, and they said over there in the U.S.A. it is easy to make a lot of money. Well, I arrived in Houston with many wishes to work. I worked hard, and I found that it is not easy to make money. The people who said that it is easy to make money in the U.S.A. did not tell the truth.

I saw that here you have many opportunities to progress, but you have to work very hard. Now, I also know that it is necessary to study. Some people on my job are bilingual and they make easy money. If not, you have to work too hard.

Javier Lares, "I Came to America," *Literacy Links*, vol. 7, Summer 2003. Reproduced by permission.

Going Nowhere

We were working for a contractor and lots of people have many years working with this contractor and this company. They don't try to study or to speak English. I decided that I don't like that for me because I have my family, in Texas and in Mexico. I like to send my family in Mexico some money every month.

With this contractor, I never had a chance to do anything. I remember when we were working from 6 A.M. to 7 P.M. I did [not] have a chance to do anything except work and work. Then in one year, I became a bricklayer. Then two years later, a person offered me more money if I would go to work with him. He was another contractor whose name was Pascual, but his job was not here in Houston. His job was in Austin, and he told me that if I knew other workers, I should tell him. I had a friend who was married. He took his wife, and he went to Austin, too.

One Step Forward, Two Steps Backward

We arrived at his apartment, and this new boss man had more workers in his apartment. Well, the next day we started to work and this job was better. I had a little free time to start to study English. I bought books.

Pascual started to make a lot of money. He had a lot of workers and he started to give me a lot of responsibility on the job. Well I appreciated him because he saw that I was a good worker.

However, when I tried to get work for myself, he didn't like that. He became excited and he didn't pay me anything for the last week. He just threw me a few dollars and some change. I picked them up, and then Pascual told me, "If you don't want to work with me, get your things and go to another place. I give you one hour to get out of here. You, too," he told my friend and his wife. Can you imagine what time it was? 8 P.M. We went to a hotel that night, and the next day, I found a job by myself for my friend and me. That was better. We had a little more money and I knew it was time for me to learn to speak English. I will never forget that time.

If you try to speak English, you can know more people. You can make more friends. Three months later, when everything was perfect on my new job, Pascual, who was angry with me, reported me to Immigration, and they sent me back to Mexico. I know Pascual reported me because before he told me to get out from his apartment, he told me, "I brought you over here, and I'm going to get you out of Austin!" Why did he do that? He is a Mexican person like me. Do you believe that? But that was o.k.; I was happy because I had not seen my family in three years. I was happy to be with my family again, and I found the person who was to become my wife. My wife-to-be gave me a reason to look ahead until I felt strong enough to go back to the U.S.A.

A Second Chance

One year later, we came back to [the] U.S.A., but not to Austin. We arrived in Houston; I say "we" because now it is my wife and me. Then I was lucky because I found work in a good company. My work schedule was from 6 a.m. to 3:30 p.m. This gave me enough time to start to study.

One year later I decided to get a house, and now I have had my home for three years. I have a family, a beautiful family, and I have a good life. I'm here trying to make progress and my wife and I are studying together. We are enrolled in classes at the elementary school; we have a good teacher who is patient with all of us. She explains things very well, and she encourages us to study on our own. My speaking and writing have improved very much.

An Austrian Bodybuilder Believes in the American Dream

Arnold Schwarzenegger

Arnold Schwarzenegger emigrated from Austria to the United States in 1968 and became an American citizen in 1983. His first international success came as a professional and competitive bodybuilder, which led to his fame as a blockbuster movie action hero. He has considered himself a member of the Republican Party since 1968; his personal involvement in American politics extends as far back as 1990, when he was appointed to the position of chairman of the President's Council on Physical Fitness and Sports. On November 17, 2003, Schwarzenegger was sworn in as governor of California, an office he currently holds. The following selection is from a speech that Schwarzenegger made in 2004 at the Republican National Convention in New York City. In it, he explained why he is grateful for the opportunities America gives to immigrants like himself.

My fellow Americans, this is an amazing moment for me. To think that a once-scrawny boy from Austria could grow up to become Governor of the State of California and then stand here—and stand here in Madison Square Garden and speak on behalf of the President of the United States. That is an immigrant's dream! It's the American dream.

You know, I was born in Europe and I've traveled all over the world, and I can tell you that there is no place, no country, that is more compassionate, more generous, more accepting, and more welcoming than the United States of America.

As long as I live—As long as I live, I will never forget the day 21 years ago when I raised my right hand and I took the

Arnold Schwarzenegger, "2004 Republican National Convention Address," in www.americanrhetoric.com, August 31, 2004.

oath of citizenship. You know how proud I was? I was so proud that I walked around with the American flag around my shoulder all day long.

Tonight, I want to talk to you about why I'm even more proud to be an American—why I am proud to be a Republican, and why I believe that this country is in good hands.

When I was a boy, the Soviets occupied part of Austria. I saw their tanks in the streets. I saw communism with my own eyes. I remember the fear we had when we had to cross into the Soviet sector. Growing up, we were told, "Don't look the soldiers in the eye. Just look straight ahead." It was common belief that the Soviet soldiers could take a man out of his own car and ship him back to the Soviet Union as slave labor.

Now my family didn't have a car—but one day we were in my uncle's car. It was near dark as we came to the Soviet checkpoint. I was a little boy. I was not an action hero back then. But I remember—I remember how scared I was that the soldiers would pull my father or my uncle out of the car and I would never see them again. My family and so many others lived in fear of the Soviet boot. Today, the world no longer fears the Soviet Union and it is because of the United States of America!

As a kid—As a kid I saw socialist—the socialist country that Austria became after the Soviets left. Now don't misunderstand me: I love Austria and I love the Austrian people. But I always knew that America was the place for me. In school, when the teacher would talk about America, I would daydream about coming here. I would daydream about living here. I would sit there and watch for hours American movies, transfixed by my heroes, like John Wayne [a movie star from the 1940s to the 1970s]. Everything about America—Everything about America seemed so big to me, so open, so possible.

Becoming a Republican

I finally arrived here in 1968. What a special day it was. I remember I arrived here with empty pockets, but full of dreams, full of determination, full of desire. The presidential campaign was in full swing. I remember watching the [Richard] Nixon and [Hubert] Humphrey presidential race on TV. A friend of mine who spoke German and English translated for me. I heard Humphrey saying things that sounded like socialism, which I had just left. But then I heard Nixon speak. Then I heard Nixon speak. He was talking about free enterprise, getting the government off your back, lowering the taxes, and strengthening the military.

Listening to Nixon speak sounded more like a breath of fresh air. I said to my friend, I said, "What party is he?" My friend said, "He's a Republican." I said, "Then I am a Republican." And I have been a Republican ever since! And trust me—And trust me in my wife's family, that's no small achievement.[1] But I am proud to be with the party of Abraham Lincoln, the party of Teddy Roosevelt, the party of Ronald Reagan and the party of George W. Bush!

The Opportunities of America

To my fellow immigrants listening tonight, I want you to know how welcome you are in this party. We Republicans admire your ambition. We encourage your dreams. We believe in you[r] future. And one thing I learned about America is that if you work hard and if you play by the rules, this country is truly open to you. You can achieve anything.

Everything I have—my career, my success, my family—I owe to America.

In this country, it doesn't make any difference where you were born. It doesn't make any difference who your parents were. It doesn't make any difference if you're like me and you couldn't even speak English until you were in your twenties.

America gave me opportunities and my immigrant dreams came true. I want other people to get the same chances I did,

1. Schwarzenegger is married to Maria Shriver, a member of the Kennedy family, who are historically staunch Democrats.

the same opportunities. And I believe they can. That's why I believe in this country. That's why I believe in this party, and that's why I believe in this president [George W. Bush].

Now, many of you out there tonight are "Republican" like me—in your hearts and in your belief. Maybe you're from Guatemala. Maybe you're from the Philippines. Maybe you're from Europe or the Ivory Coast. Maybe you live in Ohio, Pennsylvania, or New Mexico. And maybe—And maybe, just maybe, you don't agree with this party on every single issue. I say to you tonight that I believe that's not only okay, but that's what's great about this country. Here—Here we can respectfully disagree and still be patriotic, still be American, and still be good Republicans. . . .

Celebrating the American Dream

We are—We are the America that sends out the Peace Corps volunteers to teach our village children. We are the America that sends out the missionaries and doctors to raise up the poor and the sick. We are the America that gives more than any other country to fight AIDS in Africa and the developing world. And we are—And we are the America that fights not for imperialism but for human rights and democracy. . . .

We are still the lamp lighting the world, especially [for] those who struggle. No matter in what labor camp they slave, no matter in what injustice they're trapped, they hear our call, they see our light, and they feel the pull of our freedom.

They come here as I did because they believe. They believe in us. They come because their hearts say to them, as mine did, "If only I can get to America." You know, someone once wrote: "There are those who say that freedom is nothing but a dream." They are right. It's the American dream. . . .

My fellow Americans, I want you to know that I believe with all my heart that America remains "the great idea" that inspires the world. It is a privilege to be born here. It is an honor to become a citizen here. It is a gift to raise your family here, to vote here, and to live here.

Organizations to Contact

American Friends Service Committee (AFSC)
1501 Cherry St., Philadelphia, PA   19102
(215) 241-7000 • fax: (215) 241-7275
e-mail: afscinfo@afsc.org
Web site: www.afsc.org/immigrants-rights

The AFSC is a Quaker organization dedicated to service, development, social justice, and peace programs throughout the world. Its Immigrants' Rights Web site educates people about immigrants' rights, maintains an archive of immigration news and policies, and provides legal referrals and assistance to immigrants who need them.

American Immigration Control Foundation (AIC Foundation)
PO Box 525, Monterey, VA   24465
(540) 468-2022 • fax: (540) 468-2024
e-mail: aicfndn@cfw.com
Web site: www.aicfoundation.com

The AIC Foundation is a research and educational organization whose primary goal is to promote a reasonable immigration policy based on national interests. The AIC Foundation educates the public on what its members believe are the disastrous effects of uncontrolled immigration. It publishes the monthly newsletter *Border Watch*, as well as several monographs and books on the historical, legal, and demographic aspects of immigration.

American Immigration Lawyers Association (AILA)
918 F St. NW, Washington, DC   20004-1400
(202) 216-2400 • fax: (202) 783-7853
Web site: www.aila.org

The AILA is a national association of attorneys and law professors who practice and teach immigration law. AILA attorneys represent U.S. families who have applied for permanent residence for their spouses, children, and other close relatives, and thousands of U.S. businesses and industries who sponsor highly skilled foreign workers seeking to enter the United States on a temporary or permanent basis. AILA attorneys also represent foreign students, entertainers, athletes, and asylum seekers. The association publishes the journal *Immigration Law Today*, the weekly news brief *Capitol Beat*, and resources for practicing immigration lawyers.

Federation for American Immigrant Reform (FAIR)
1666 Connecticut Ave. NW, Suite 400
Washington, DC 20009
(202) 328-7004 • fax: (202) 387-3447
Web site: www.fairus.org

FAIR is a national organization of citizens who share a common belief that U.S. immigration policies must be reformed. Its members seek to improve border security, stop illegal immigration, and establish immigration levels at about three hundred thousand people a year.

Immigrant Legal Resource Center (ILRC)
1663 Mission St., Suite 602, San Francisco, CA 94103
(415) 255-9499
Web site: www.ilrc.org

The ILRC works with immigrants and citizens to make critical legal assistance and social services accessible to everyone, regardless of income, and to build a society that values diversity and respects the dignity and rights of all people. The ILRC develops leadership by encouraging immigrants to take on roles confronting and reshaping the laws and policies that perpetuate racial, economic, and social injustice.

Immigrant Magazine
3272 Motor Ave., Suite J, Los Angeles, CA   90034
(310) 559-9994 • fax: (310) 559-8520
e-mail: publisher@immigrantmagazine.com
Web site: www.immigrantmagazine.com

Immigrant Magazine provides its immigrant audience with online publications that will enhance their experience in the United States and forums that address their unique concerns and interests. By connecting immigrants to one another and to the rest of the nation, the magazine increases understanding, encourages tolerance, provokes thought, promotes discussion, creates opportunity, and ultimately helps provide an improved appreciation of America's rich ethnic heritage.

Immigrants Support Network (ISN)
PO Box 177, Budd Lake, NJ   07828
(509) 278-2582
e-mail: liaison@isn.org

ISN is a nonprofit, international organization that supports people trying to legally immigrate to the United States through the employment channel. It acts as an interface between prospective immigrants and the U.S. government and tries to eliminate procedural hurdles that affect the immigration process.

International Immigrants Foundation (IIF)
7 West 44th St., New York, NY   10036
(212) 302-2222 • fax: (212) 204-1294
e-mail: iif@10.org
Web site: www.10.org

The mission of the IIF is to help immigrant families and children achieve their aspirations for a better life in the United States. The organization provides direct support to promote positive intercultural relations. IIF has consultative status with the United Nations Economic and Social Council and is associated with the Department of Public Information as a charitable nongovernmental, nonpolitical, nonprofit organization.

Migration Policy Institute (MPI)
1400 16th St. NW, Suite 300, Washington, DC   20036
(202) 266-1940 • fax: (202) 266-1900
Web site: www.migrationpolicy.org

MPI is an independent, nonpartisan, nonprofit think tank in Washington, D.C. It is dedicated to the study of the migration patterns of people worldwide. MPI provides analysis, development, and evaluation of migration and refugee policies at local, national, and international levels. It aims to meet the rising demand for pragmatic and thoughtful responses to the challenges and opportunities that large-scale migration—voluntary or forced—presents to communities and institutions in an increasingly integrated world. Its Web site, the Migration Information Source, offers current and authoritative data on international migration as well as analysis from migration experts and dispatches from foreign correspondents around the world.

Minuteman Project, Inc.
PO Box 3944, Laguna Hills, CA   92654-3944
(949) 222-4266 • fax: (949) 222-6607
e-mail: info@minutemanproject.com
Web site: www.minutemanproject.com

The Minuteman Project seeks to bring national awareness to deficiencies in the local, state, and federal enforcement of U.S. immigration law. Its members emphasize that the nation is governed by the "rule of law" and not by the desires of immigrants who illegally cross the border.

National Immigration Forum (NIF)
50 F St. NW, Suite 300, Washington, DC   20001
(202) 347-0040 • fax: (202) 347-0058
Web site: www.immigrationforum.org

The NIF believes that legal immigrants strengthen America. It supports effective measures aimed at curbing illegal immigration and promotes programs and policies that help refugees and immigrants assimilate into American society. NIF publishes the quarterly newsletter *Golden Door* and the bimonthly newsletter *Immigration Policy Matters.*

National Immigration Law Center (NILC)

3435 Wilshire Blvd., Suite 2850, Los Angeles, CA   90010
(213) 639-3900 • fax: (213) 639-3911
e-mail: info@nilc.org
Web site: www.nilc.org

NILC protects and promotes the rights and opportunities of low-income immigrants and their family members. NILC staff specialize in immigration law and the employment and public benefits rights of immigrants, and provide advice and trainings to legal aid agencies, community groups, and attorneys. It publishes the *Immigrants' Rights Update* newsletter.

National Network for Immigrant and Refugee Rights (NNIRR)

310 Eighth St., Suite 303, Oakland, CA   94607
(510) 465-1984 • fax: (510) 465-1885
e-mail: nnirr@nnirr.org
Web site: www.nnirr.org

The NNIRR includes community, church, labor, and legal groups committed to the cause of equal rights for all immigrants. These groups work to end discrimination and unfair treatment of illegal immigrants and refugees. It publishes a monthly newsletter, *Network News.*

Office of Refugee Resettlement, U.S. Department of Health and Human Services (ORR)

370 L'Enfant Promenade SW, 6th Floor East
Washington, DC   20447
(202) 401-9246 • fax: (202) 401-5487
Web site: www.acf.hhs.gov/programs/orr

The ORR helps refugees, asylum seekers, and other immigrants to establish a new life founded on the dignity of economic self-support. It funds and facilitates a variety of programs that offer, among other benefits and services, cash and medical assistance, employment preparation and job placement, skills training, English language training, social adjustment, and aid for victims of torture.

U.S. Citizenship and Immigration Services, U.S. Department of Homeland Security (USCIS)

20 Massachusetts Ave. NW, Washington, DC   20529
(800) 375-5283
Web site: www.uscis.gov

USCIS allows the Department of Homeland Security to improve the administration of benefits and immigration services for applicants by exclusively focusing on immigration and citizenship services. USCIS processes all immigrant and nonimmigrant benefits provided to visitors of the United States.

U.S. Committee for Refugees and Immigrants (USCRI)

1717 Massachusetts Ave. NW, 2nd Floor
Washington, DC   20036-2003
(202) 347-3507 • fax: (202) 347-3418
Web site: www.refugees.org

The USCRI addresses the needs and rights of persons in forced or voluntary migration worldwide by advancing fair and humane public policy, facilitating and providing direct professional services, and promoting the full participation of migrants in community life. It also works with a nationwide network of state and local governments and other agencies to provide immigrants with services from the first days of their arrival, from finding employment to purchasing a home and in other ways successfully participating in the United States. The USCRI also runs the National Center for Refugee and Immigrant Children.

For Further Research

Books

Roni Berger, *Immigrant Women Tell Their Stories*. Binghamton, NY: Haworth, 2004.

Judith M. Blohm and Terri Lapinsky, *Kids Like Me: Voices of the Immigrant Experience*. Boston: Intercultural Press, 2006.

Janet Bode, *The Colors of Freedom: Immigrant Stories*. New York: Franklin Watts, 1999.

Elizabeth Boosahda, *Arab-American Faces and Voices: The Origins of an Immigrant Community*. Austin: University of Texas Press, 2003.

Ilona Bray, *U.S. Immigration Made Easy*. Berkeley, CA: Nolo, 2006.

Marina Tamar Budhos, *Remix: Conversations with Immigrant Teenagers*. New York: Holt, 1999.

William A.V. Clark, *Immigrants and the American Dream: Remaking the Middle Class*. New York: Guilford, 2003.

Roger Daniels, *Guarding the Golden Door: American Immigration Policy and Immigrants Since 1882*. New York: Hill & Wang, 2004.

Donald R. Gallo, ed., *First Crossing: Stories About Teen Immigrants*. Cambridge, MA: Candlewick, 2004.

Cristina Igoa, *The Inner World of the Immigrant Child*. Mahwah, NJ: Lawrence Erlbaum, 1995.

Stacy J. Lee, *Up Against Whiteness: Race, School, and Immigrant Youth*. New York: Teachers College Press, 2005.

Ann V. Millard and Jorge Chapa, *Apple Pie and Enchiladas: Latino Newcomers in the Rural Midwest*. Austin: University of Texas Press, 2004.

Laurie Olsen, *Made in America: Immigrant Students in Our Public Schools*. New York: New Press, 1997.

Alejandro Portes and Ruben G. Rumbaut, *Legacies: The Story of the Immigrant Second Generation*. Berkeley: University of California Press, 2001.

Ruben G. Rumbaut and Alejandro Portes, eds., *Ethnicities: Children of Immigrants in America*. Berkeley: University of California Press, 2001.

Carola Suarez-Orozco and Marcelo M. Suarez-Orozco, *Children of Immigration*. Cambridge, MA: Harvard University Press, 2001.

May Paomay Tung, *Chinese Americans and Their Immigrant Parents: Conflict, Identity, and Values*. Binghamton, NY: Haworth, 2000.

Periodicals

Lorraine Ali, "Islam: A New Welcoming Spirit in the Mosque," *Newsweek*, August 29, 2005.

Behrooz Arshadi, "Treated Like a Criminal: How the INS Stole Three Days of My Life," *Progressive*, March 2003.

Alvaro Bedoya, "Captive Labor: The Plight of Peruvian Sheepherders Illuminates Broader Exploitation of Immigrant Workers in U.S. Agriculture," *Dollars & Sense*, September–October 2003.

Dina Berta, "Greek Immigrant Builds Lifetime Career with Empire of Restaurants in Denver," *Nation's Restaurant News*, March 6, 2006.

Steven A. Camarota and Mark Krikorian, "A Myth Dies Hard: Little Evidence Found That Immigrants Are Entrepreneurial," *National Review*, February 21, 2000.

Arian Campo-Flores, "'Macho' or 'Sweetness'? A New Harvard Study Shows That Immigrant Boys and Girls Fare Very Differently in the Outside World," *Newsweek*, July 1, 2002.

Jeff Chu and Nadia Mustafa, "Between Two Worlds: Born in the U.S.A. to Asian Parents, a Generation of Immigrants' Kids Forges a New Identity," *Time*, January 16, 2006.

Leila Cobo, "Los Tigres Take Their Stories from Real Life; Songs Focus on Immigration Issues, Juarez Deaths," *Billboard*, April 17, 2004.

Marcia Coyle, "As Skaters Take Silver, Their Lawyers Get Gold," *National Law Journal*, February 27, 2006.

John Derbyshire, "The Straggler: I Was an Illegal Alien," *National Review*, March 24, 2003.

Economist, "Into the Suburbs: Immigration," March 13, 2004.

———, "Perilous Crossing: Cuba," November 5, 2005.

Maggie Jones, "The New Yankees: Before the Somali Refugees Showed Up, Lewiston, Maine, Was Just Another Struggling Mill Town," *Mother Jones*, March–April 2004.

Danielle Knight, "Waiting in Limbo, Their Childhood Lost," *U.S. News & World Report*, March 15, 2004.

Karen E. Lange, "Home Far Away: 02860," *National Geographic*, June 2004.

James Lardner, "Give Us Your Wired Elite: Immigrant Computer Engineers," *U.S. News & World Report*, July 10, 2000.

Luis Fernando Llosa, "Going Native," *Sports Illustrated*, May 8, 2006.

Michael Luongo, "Love Overseas: A Host of Legal Problems Can Ensue When You Try to Bring a Foreign-Born Partner Back Home to the United States," *Advocate*, March 1, 2005.

Michael Mandel, "The Melting Pot Is Still Melting: Unlike Their Counterparts in France, U.S. Immigrants Are Getting Ahead," *Business Week*, December 12, 2005.

Mary Jo McConahay, "No Place to Call Home: Immigrants Running from Environmental Disasters," *Sierra*, November 2000.

John J. Miller, "Immigrants for President: Why the Foreign-Born Should Be Allowed to Compete for the Big Job," *National Review*, August 6, 2001.

Liza Monroy, "In the 'Barn' I Realized Just How Lucky I Am," *Newsweek*, March 27, 2006.

Charles W. Petit, "Foreign Scholars in Visa Limbo," *U.S. News & World Report*, October 13, 2003.

Jonathan Pont, "From Immigrant Outsider to D.C. Insider: Elaine Chao," *Workforce Management*, August 1, 2005.

Bill Powell, "Running out of the Darkness," *Time*, May 1, 2006.

Helene Slessarev-Jamir, "Looking for Welcome: Fearful of Harsh Border Enforcement Legislation and Trapped in Poverty, Many Immigrants Turn to Churches for Help," *Sojourners*, April 2006.

Mark Steyn, "In 'the Same Boat,' Up a Creek," *National Review*, May 22, 2006.

Pat McDonnell Twair, "Their American Dream Became a Nightmare," *Middle East*, June 2005.

Richard Weissbourd, "Down Home: The Problem with Becoming American," *New Republic*, February 25, 2002.

Mortimer B. Zuckerman, "Land of Opportunity," *U.S. News & World Report*, June 20, 2005.

Index